In the
Middle
of the
Night

Robert Cormier

Delacorte  Press

Published by
Delacorte Press
Bantam Doubleday Dell Publishing Group, Inc.
1540 Broadway
New York, New York 10036

Library of Congress Cataloging-in-Publication Data

Cormier, Robert.
    In the middle of the night / by Robert Cormier.
      p.   cm.
    Summary: Sixteen-year-old Denny lives in the shadow of a deadly accident with
which his father was connected when he was Denny's age, a disaster for which
some of the survivors still blame his father.
    ISBN 0-385-32158-9
    [1. Revenge—Fiction.   2. Mystery and detective stories.]
    I. Title.
PZ7.C816534In   1995
[Fic]—dc20   94-38894   CIP   AC

The text of this book is set in 12-point Berkeley Book.

Book design by Sheree Goodman

Manufactured in the United States of America

May 1995

10 9 8 7 6 5 4

TO THE GRANDCHILDREN

Jennifer Sullivan
Travis, Darren and Mallory Cormier
Emily, Claire, Sam and Drew Hayes
Ellen and Amy Wheeler

With Love

Me and my sister. My sister and me. Sustaining each other through the years, although we often argued about what she insists on doing. The telephone calls, for instance. I have allowed them, without approving of them. But now she wants to call the boy, instead of the father.

I am writing all this down. I have never kept a diary or a journal or anything like that. My thoughts and memories were enough, but now that she has begun to assert herself, I find that it's necessary to keep a record. Why? For my own good, my own testimony, in case anything happens.

Stop pretending, she says. *You know what's going to happen.*

I ignore her. I don't answer.

Don't you? she asks.

Don't I what? Answering her but not wanting to be

drawn into her plans, and knowing that I won't be able to resist.

Don't you know what's going to happen? Think of what happened to me. I'm the one who went through it all.

My sister's name is Louise but everyone always calls her Lulu because she couldn't pronounce Louise properly when she was a baby. It came out something like Lulu.

We've always spent a lot of time together. Even though she is less than a year older, she treats me as if I am a baby. She used to call me Baby-Boy and still calls me Baby.

Even as a kid she acted like she was my mother. She loved to touch me. Tickle me or caress me. She would grab and poke and massage me, and this would drive me crazy. I'd begin to giggle, then laugh, and then get sick to my stomach.

Stop, stop, I'd cry, and she would finally stop and take me in her arms and hold me, kissing my cheeks, wet kisses, sometimes tears in the kisses, and she'd tell me how much she loved me.

I will take care of you forever, Baby, she'd say. *I will never leave you.*

And I believed her.

We went to live with Aunt Mary after our parents died. Aunt Mary was my mother's sister. She never married and taught second grade at St. Luke's Parochial School. She stopped in at St. Luke's Church next to the school every day after classes. She said three rosaries every night before she went to bed, kneeling on the floor. She ran the household like she ran her classes, a time set aside to do everything. *Our time* was from seven to eight o'clock. She devoted that hour to Lulu and me, and we devoted it to her. We would read books out loud or put on small plays for her that Lulu made up. The plays were mostly her versions of movies or television shows. Like the final scene in an old movie called *Wuthering Heights* where she was Cathy dying in bed and I was Heathcliff and had to pick her up after she died and carry her to the window. My legs always buckled when I picked her up and she'd get mad at me and I'd get mad at her because I didn't want her to die, even in a play. Sometimes she'd switch to comedy because she liked to see Aunt Mary laugh. Aunt Mary did not laugh often and Lulu was delighted when Aunt Mary suddenly yelped with laughter. Mostly she laughed when Lulu presented her version of *I Love Lucy*. She played Lucy, of course, and I was Ricky Ricardo and she made me practice his accent.

Aunt Mary was our mother and father and all our aunts and uncles put together. There was no one else in our family but the three of us. Our mother and father died when we were very young. I can't remember them at all, although Lulu claims she can. Times when I was feeling sad, she'd tell me stories about them. How they loved to dance. How they'd turn on the radio or put a record on the phonograph and dance in the kitchen and float through the rooms in each other's arms, gliding over the linoleum in the kitchen, almost as if their feet weren't touching the floor.

How can you remember that, I asked, *if I can't?*

I guess because I'm brighter than you, she said.

3

But you were two years old when they died.

A smart two-year-old, she said. *Know what? I remember popping out. I remember the slap. Right on my bottom. Hurt like hell . . .* And she laughed.

I never knew whether she was making up stories or not, but I loved to hear her tell about our mother and father dancing through the rooms of the apartment.

Their favorite song was Elvis Presley's "Blue Christmas." Everybody else played Bing Crosby's "White Christmas," but they put on "Blue Christmas" and danced around the room.

But "Blue Christmas" is a sad song, I said. *Sad words, sad music.*

"White Christmas" isn't a barrel of laughs, either, she said. *Maybe they liked sad songs because they had an inkling about what was going to happen to them.*

I envied Lulu because she remembered so much. And even if she was only pretending, I envied her ability to make it seem real.

We lived on the second floor below the Denehans and their six children. Eileen Denehan was Lulu's best friend. I was not best friends with any of the Denehans. They were loud and lively, running all over the place, but none of them liked to read or ever went near the library. Eileen's brothers—Billy, Kevin, Mickey, Raymond and Tom—played baseball, and Lulu joked that they should take up basketball and have a team of their own. They ignored me and I never looked at them. Anyway, I had Lulu. And Lulu had me. But she also had Eileen. Eileen was the brightest of them all, and the liveliest.

Like Lulu. They could finish each other's sentences and they loved ridiculous talking-animal jokes, making them up, jokes that were funny only to them. Why does a kangaroo say ouch? Answer: Pouch. I think their ridiculous jokes were some kind of code, but I never asked Lulu about that.

Eileen told us about the big Halloween show at the Globe Theater. Magic acts and singers and dancers and jugglers and one year a man who walked on a wire high above the heads of the kids in the audience. *But there are only so many seats,* she said. *And you have to be impoverished to be eligible for a ticket.*

What's impoverished? Eileen's brother Billy asked.

Poor, Eileen said.

I know what impoverished *means and we're not impoverished,* Lulu said.

Yes you are, Eileen said in her know-it-all manner, which matched Lulu's. Which is why they were such good friends.

My idea of fun isn't going to a show with a thousand screaming kids, Lulu said.

Then she saw my face. I liked the idea of seeing a magician perform tricks live onstage and not just in the movies.

Okay, Lulu said, *if we have to be impoverished to see this show, then that's what we will be.*

Later, in our seven-to-eight time with Aunt Mary, Lulu said: *I know we're not really impoverished, but there's this Hal-*

loween show we'd like to see that Eileen upstairs told us about.

Oh, I know about that show, Aunt Mary said. *It's a tradition here in Wickburg. Why didn't I think of it before, having you both go to the show?* She began to cry.

See what you're missing with an old maid bringing you up? Tears on her cheeks now like small soap bubbles that had burst. *You don't have to be impoverished to go, and you're both eligible. Because you're orphans, poor things.* Really crying now, her cheeks messy and her nose running. Lulu handed her a Kleenex.

We were orphans, all right, Lulu and me.

We were barely two when my mother and father went to the drive-in theater one night. They usually did not go to drive-in theaters because that's where the horror movies were shown and young couples made out in cars, and wise guys threw popcorn around and drank beer while sitting on the hoods of their cars. But my father was a sentimental one, Aunt Mary said. My mother and father went to a drive-in on their first date and he talked my mother into going again, for old times' sake. But the wise guys were wiser than ever that night, drunk or maybe high. They gathered around my parents' car and began to shake it back and forth and bang on the hood and my father put down the windows and swore at them, and finally drove out of there. But the wise guys followed in their cars—two or three of them—and chased them down Route 2, bumping them from behind and cutting in front of them. My father lost control and his car smashed into a tree. Looked like a busted accordion, Lulu said.

She claimed she remembered the night they went to that drive-in, how my mother wore a blue dress with sequins like she was going to a fancy ball and my father wore a white shirt and his best tie, blue with red stripes. They looked beautiful and happy, Lulu said, and that's a good thing to remember. But I think she only told me that to make me feel good.

Anyway, that's how we became orphans and went to live with Aunt Mary.

Lulu never liked to ride in buses. She could not stand the smell of exhaust which always seemed to her to seep up through the floor, so it did not matter whether the windows were opened or closed.

The bus was crowded, everyone but Lulu excited over the prospect of the show at the Globe with a magician who, they said, made people disappear. Everyone was talking at once, and three or four kids were singing some silly song about a duck. Lulu and Eileen and I were crammed together, me in the middle, in one seat. Eileen ignored me as usual, and so did her brothers. They kept running up and down the aisles, paying no attention to the pleas of the driver to please sit down everybody. Eileen could not believe that I had taken a book along, a paperback I had slipped into my pocket and thought nobody had noticed. I always carried a book with me wherever I went.

When we arrived at the Globe, a huge sign in front of the theater showed an evil-looking magician whose hands dripped with blood. Everybody on the bus, even the Denehans, were awestruck and silent.

7

Single file, the bus driver called out, and everyone obeyed. Lulu held my hand even though I was walking behind her.

Got your coupons? Lulu asked, looking at me over her shoulder. I nodded: coupons for free candy and soda pop —naturally I had them safe in my pocket.

Inside, Lulu dispatched me to find three good seats while she took my coupons. *Chocolate,* I told her in case some kind of ice cream was involved.

I pushed and pulled my way through kids running every which way, yelling and laughing, and found three seats about halfway down from the stage. There would be no possibility of reading my book until Lulu showed up because I had to defend the seats from kids looking for their own seats: *These are saved,* I said a thousand times.

The Globe was an old theater, not like those at the shopping center, and kids pointed up at the big chandelier, all frozen glass and gold, reminding me of a stalactite. But the bulbs were not lit and the chandelier hung there, suspended by a wire that looked very thin and threadlike.

Lulu saw me looking up at the chandelier.

Don't be nervous, she said.

But I couldn't help being nervous and Lulu could always read my mind.

That chandelier makes me nervous, too, Eileen said. She looked around and summoned Billy and Kevin. Their cheeks were scarlet and their red hair disheveled from all their activities.

Find us three seats away from here, Eileen commanded.

Off they went, pushing and shoving, crowding other kids out of the way. We stood there in the middle of that

8

pandemonium, Lulu and Eileen munching popcorn, their lips wet with butter while my ice cream melted on the cone, oozing over my fingers. *They had no napkins,* Lulu said, disgusted, wiping her mouth with the back of her hand.

Finally, Billy beckoned us. He had probably used strong-arm tactics, but one way or another he had found us seats three-quarters of the way from the stage, side by side, under the balcony.

It's pretty far from the stage, I complained.

Lulu gave me her patient look.

We all sat down together.

Ten minutes later, Lulu was dead.

And the nightmare began.

Part One

Part One

*T*he ringing telephone blistered the night, stripping him of sleep, like a bandage torn from flesh. He looked toward the digital clock: 3:18 in vivid scarlet numbers. Instantly alert, he thought: it's beginning again, but too early—much too early this year.

The first call usually came sometime in October, a week or two before the anniversary. This, however, was early September, in the final hours of a lingering heat wave. Fans turned lazily in the bedroom windows, fans that did not blur the sound of the telephone, incessant and insistent. Please make it a wrong number, he prayed.

Raising himself on one elbow, he listened, counting the rings, pausing after each one . . . six (pause), seven (pause) . . . and heard his father padding wearily down the hallway. Did not actually hear his father but *felt* him proceeding slowly, reluctantly, but going all the same.

The telephone's ringing ended abruptly.

He waited, still half-sitting, half-lying, his elbow jammed into the mattress. Perspiration dampened his forehead. He strained to listen, heard nothing. Finally, he got out of bed and walked carefully to the door—his door was always open a crack—and, squinting, saw his father, his white shorts and T-shirt stamped against the darkness, standing with the telephone to his ear, listening. He watched him for long moments, not daring to move.

His father put down the telephone and stood there, mute and alone and still.

Denny knew then that it had not been a wrong number. He stared at his father as his father stared at the phone. Sighing softly, Denny turned and made his way back to the bed, eyes getting accustomed to the darkness now, shape and sizes assuming identity—CD player, desk upon which he did his homework, bulletin board—all of it stark, impersonal, like a hotel room. Chilly suddenly, he snapped off the window fan.

He stood at the window, looking out at the quiet street, subdued in shadows, the maple tree across the street like a giant ink blot. The windows of the other apartment buildings were dark. Down the street, a splash of light from the 24-Hour Store. He wondered what kind of person shopped at three o'clock in the morning. Or used a telephone at that hour.

Back in bed, finally, he tried to relax and bring on sleep. He tossed and turned, the sheet entangling his legs. Thinking of that terrible October date a few weeks away, he vowed that this time he wouldn't stand by like his father and do nothing. He wasn't a little kid anymore. He was sixteen. He didn't know what he would do, but he would do *something*.

"I'm not my father," he muttered into his pillow.

Sleep took a long time coming.

I hear her restless in the night, walking the floor, pacing up and down. I don't move in my bed, pretending I'm asleep. I know what she wants to do. I know that she wants to call him. I hope she doesn't. But I also know that Halloween is coming and she must call.

She always stands by my bed before calling. Making sure I'm asleep. I try to make my breathing regular. I fake snoring, not too much because then she'll know I'm trying to fool her. What I want to say is: Please don't call. Leave him alone. But it's futile. Especially this year.

Last night, she went through the routine again. Pacing up and down, standing at the window looking out, then beside my bed.

I heard her punching the numbers on the phone. That eerie tune the Touch-Tone plays. I heard her voice. Quiet at first, gentle. Then harsh as she got angry, as she always does.

Why does he listen? I wonder. Why doesn't he hang up? Why doesn't he take the phone off the hook at night? Or have it taken out?

What does he say to you? I asked her once.

Nothing, she said. *He just listens. But I can almost hear his heart beating.*

Last night was different, though. She did not become angry and her voice was almost tender as she spoke to him.

When she hung up, she came and stood beside my bed. I knew she was there because I heard the soft slap of her slippers on the floor as she approached.

I opened my eyes and looked up at her.

I won't call him anymore, she said.

A sigh escaped me, like a ghost abandoning my body.

Now it's the son, she said. *The sin of the father will be visited upon the son.*

Oh no, Lulu, I said. *Please don't do that.*

I have to do it, she said.

No you don't.

I was the one who died, she said, *not you.*

She turned away from me, letting herself be swallowed up in the nighttime gloom.

*T*he usual morning scene: Denny, his mother and his father.

His mother at the stove, waiting for the coffee to bubble in the little glass knob of the percolator; his father with the newspaper in front of him, rippling the pages as he turns them; Denny eating the tasteless shredded wheat like trying to swallow hay.

Back to his mother: still pretty but in a fading way, turning pastel. Streaks of gray lacing her still blond hair. Her skin like ivory, pale. Everything about her pale except for her eyes. Brown-black, sharp, radiant. Her best feature, she always says, although she has never done anything to enhance them.

He always checked his mother's eyes when he wanted to confirm what she was really thinking. She was always aware of what he was doing, though it remained unspoken between them. When she'd turn away, he'd know instinctively that she was hiding something from him. Most often it had to do with his father.

His father. Behind the newspaper. *Hiding* behind the newspaper, especially this morning. Was he really reading the paper? He never discussed what he read in the paper. Did not react. The Red Sox lose another ball game, blowing it in the final inning? No reaction. Another senseless death on the streets over in Boston? A beating? A drive-by shooting? A gang rape? No reaction. Did he actually read the paper or was he only using it as a barricade?

Himself. What did his mother and father see when they looked at him? The obvious: dutiful son, good student —not brilliant, not a genius (definitely not a genius), but a regular kid. Did not give them cause for alarm. Polite. Oh, sarcastic sometimes when things piled up and no one spoke or said anything. Uncoordinated, awkward at sports, quiet. Spent a lot of time in his room. Reading, mostly junk but some good junk, too—the 87th Precinct novels he was racing through.

That's what someone would see, peeking in the window: a regular family. Breakfast time. Mother at the stove. Father reading the newspaper. Son dutifully eating the dreaded shredded wheat because his mother said it was good for him.

But anyone looking in would not know about the telephone call.

He pushed the bowl away. The coffee began to percolate. His father ruffled the paper to show that he had not finished reading it. If he lowered the newspaper, he would encounter his son, his wife.

Denny had been in the kitchen for fifteen minutes and nobody had said anything except "good morning." They seldom spoke much as a family, particularly at breakfast. His father preferred silence to a lot of talking and his mother took her cue from him. The silences were comfortable most of the time. This morning's silence was different, however, and he wanted to break it.

Which is exactly what he did, finally.

"I heard the phone ring during the night."

Dropped the words on the table, like stones striking a surface.

The newspaper trembled in his father's hands.

"Or was I dreaming?" Hoping his father caught the sarcasm.

More silence. More waiting. Then more sarcasm:

"Or was it a wrong number?"

He was tired of pretense, silences, a "failure to communicate" (a phrase he'd heard in an old late-night movie on television).

Finally, his father spoke from behind the newspaper. "It was not a wrong number." He lowered the newspaper and began to fold it, slowly and methodically.

His father was a small slender man, compact, neat. Shoes always shined, shirt never wrinkled. He could fool around with a car engine or work outside and never soil his clothes. Never a dab of dirt or grease on his face. Denny attracted dirt and grime, and his shirts and trousers began to wrinkle the moment he put them on, before he'd even taken a step.

"The telephone rang at exactly three-eighteen," his father said, in his formal precise manner. He seldom used slang. Spoke as if he was trying out the words for the first time. He was still folding the newspaper, had not raised his eyes to either Denny or his wife.

Denny waited for his father to say more, but his father signaled for his coffee to be poured. His mother didn't look at Denny. She didn't look at his father, either, concentrating on serving the coffee as if she were conducting some important experiment in pouring.

Denny took a deep breath and plunged. This year, this time, had to be different.

"So it's started again," he said.

His father smiled, a wisp of a smile, the saddest smile Denny had ever seen. In fact, not a smile at all but a mere alteration of his expression.

"Again," his father said, nodding heavily, as if his head was too heavy for his shoulders.

His mother spoke from the sink. "This year, we ought to take the phone out. Or at least change the number. Unlisted. Unpublished."

His father looked at his mother. Denny knew that look. Knew what it meant. *We are not taking the phone out.*

"Especially this year," she said, turning and meeting his eyes.

"It's just another year, Nina," his father said.

"No it isn't." Her face grim, determined. Which surprised Denny because his mother was usually quick to agree with his father, always willing to smooth things over.

He hated to see his parents at odds with each other. He had never really seen them argue except about this one

21

thing. Even then the argument mostly took the form of silences. But certain silences, he'd found, could be worse than yelling and shouting.

She ran the faucet. "We hardly use the phone anyway. How many people know us here? How many other people call us?"

Other people. Terrible words that emphasized who really called them.

His father said: "We keep the phone. And we are not going to move anymore. We found this place, it's nice, and we are staying. No more moving." He looked at Denny's mother, then at Denny, then back to Denny's mother. "So, everything stays the same."

Brave words. Denny wanted to cheer his father on. But the moment passed and he pressed his lips together, thinking of all the nights ahead and all the telephone calls to come. Along with everything else.

Everything else, he thought, as he made his way through the warmth of the sunny morning to the bus stop. Meaning: the letters his father barely read before either burning them in the sink or flushing them down the toilet; reporters ringing the doorbell; the newspapers with his father's name in headlines along with that old picture of him as a boy; his father's face flashing on television. Not all the time, of course, and not every year. But certainly this year, a special year, the twenty-fifth-anniversary year.

Arriving at the bus stop, he looked dismally at the kids waiting there. Humiliating, starting every school day like this, the only high-school student in the neighborhood. The others at the bus stop were elementary-school students, the oldest sixth-graders, some of them younger. It was a maverick bus, picking up unassigned and stray students.

"Hey, Denny, when are you gonna get a car and drive us all to school?"

Same old questions every day from Dracula, to whom Denny had confessed one day that his father wouldn't allow him to get his license until he was seventeen. Too many crazy teenagers on the road, his father said. Denny had planned to wage a campaign for the license, to get it *now* and not wait. But that telephone call and all it meant complicated the situation.

"Hey, Denny, you need a license before you get a car, right?" Dracula persisted.

Denny ignored him. Ignored the other kids, too. Unruly kids, scuffling, fighting, filling the air with four-letter words. As usual, a couple of them started to fight. Frankenstein and The Wolfman this time. He had private names for all of them, most of them movie monsters. Even the small third-grader who was always getting pushed around by the older kids. Denny called him Son of Frankenstein, because he could be a pain, too, at any given moment.

Frankenstein and The Wolfman were really going at it now, grappling and scuffling and falling to the ground. Denny watched without emotion.

"Why don't you do something?"

He turned at the words to confront a girl whose eyes were flashing with anger. She looked at him with the same kind of disgust he reserved for the little monsters. "They're going to kill each other . . ."

"So—let them kill each other," he said. But did not mean what he said, of course, letting his anger toward the kids, the girl, himself, come to the surface. Who was this girl to challenge him like that? He didn't care if she was pretty or not. Actually, she was beautiful.

Shaking her head in disgust, she proceeded to stop the fight. She put down her bookbag, and began to tug at The Wolfman, who was on top of Frankenstein. While Dracula and Ygor and everybody else cheered them on.

Denny watched, astonished, as the girl wrenched The Wolfman away from Frankenstein and swung him around by the shoulders. When she let go, he tumbled to the sidewalk in a yelp of pain and humiliation.

She bent over Frankenstein. "Are you okay?" she asked.

He kicked out at her. "Let me alone, bitch," he yelled, scuttling away.

The girl picked up her bookbag and looked toward Denny. "Thanks for all your help," she said, voice dry as playground sand.

"You didn't seem to need any," he said.

Two other kids started pushing and shoving, calling each other names.

"See?" he said to her. "It's like a war. You win one battle but the war goes on . . ." He thought that sounded pretty clever.

She did not reply. She walked to the other end of the bus stop. Surreptitiously, he glanced at her. Her blue bookbag hung from her shoulder. Her hair was as black as midnight. She wore a white blouse and a beige skirt.

On the bus, he sat alone as usual.

He was surprised when she sat down beside him. There were plenty of empty seats; she could have sat anywhere.

"Mind?" she asked, but already settling in.

"Free country," he said, shrugging, his pulse leaping in his temple.

"Thank you." Was she being sarcastic?

The bus lurched to a start. One of the little monsters slid off his seat and landed on the floor with a yelp. He was cheered and jeered.

"Why do you look so sour?" the girl asked.

"What?" he replied, startled. Did he actually look sour?

"I said: You look sour. What do you see out the window that makes you so sour?"

"The trees," he said. Having to say something.

"Trees?"

"Right. Look at them out there. Mutilated. The power company cuts the branches, hacks away at them, so that they don't interfere with the wires. The trees all look . . . wounded."

"But the wires bring electricity to the houses," she said.

He shrugged, did not bother to answer. Was in no mood to argue.

"Would you rather be without electricity?" she asked. "Stumble around in the dark? Use candles instead of lightbulbs?"

The bus stopped for more passengers, doors opened and closed, exhaust smells filled the air.

They should bury the wires. That would protect the

trees. Also would prevent limbs coming down during storms and interrupting the power. Made sense, didn't it? But he did not say any of this to the girl. Did not want further conversation.

"Well?" she said. Was she waiting for his reply?

"Look, what do you want from me?" Still not looking at her. Heat filled the bus. Hot for September.

"Nothing," she said. "I don't want anything from you. Except perhaps a bit of civility."

Civility. Such an odd word to use in conversation. Meaning: Be civil, be civilized. Be nice.

Actually, he wanted to be nice. Wanted to be charming and witty and clever. She was beautiful in a way that made him ache. He could smell her perfume. Not perfume really but a clean outdoors kind of smell. Reminded him of breezes rippling across a pond. Miserably, he concentrated on the scenery outside the window. Not scenery at all but buildings and stores and commuter traffic. People hurrying along the sidewalk, going to their jobs. Inhaling the girl's scent, he thought of Chloe. Hadn't thought of her for weeks. Angry at himself now for thinking of her, angry at this girl for making him think of Chloe.

"What's the matter?" she asked.

He shook his head, not daring to answer, not trusting himself to speak.

She did not press him to talk. Did not ask any more questions or make any attempt at further conversation. He kept looking out the window.

The bus stopped at Barstow High. She rose from the seat, slung her bookbag over her shoulder. She stood there, looked down at him in an attitude of waiting. Waiting for what?

"Hey," she said.

He glanced up at her, caught her eyes, which were not crackling with anger like at the bus stop but soft, her expression gentle.

"I think that's kind of nice."

What's kind of nice, he wondered, mystified.

"That you worry about the trees."

And she was gone, making her way down the aisle and out the door, ignoring the shouts and whistles of the little monsters. He settled back in his seat, waiting to be dropped off at Normal Prep.

Normal Prep.

It was the nickname for Norman Preparatory Academy, named for Samuel J. Norman, a deceased Barstow millionaire, whose former home, a three-story mansion, now served as the academy's administration building. It was so damn normal, which is exactly what Denny liked about it. And hated about it. Both at the same time.

The school looked almost *too* normal: two classroom buildings, located at right angles to the mansion, bright red brick with clinging climbing ivy, two stories in height. The lawn between the buildings was mowed to such perfection that it resembled artificial turf, although no one would dare play football on its surface or even walk across it. An iron gate guarded the entrance to the academy.

The students, all boys, wore navy blue blazers and gray trousers, the official school uniform. Students were allowed to wear shirts and ties of their own choosing although the official Norman catalog asked that these be "tasteful in design and color."

Denny's father was enthusiastic about Norman Prep, even though the tuition meant that he had to work overtime at the factory to earn extra money. He said he wanted the best possible education for Denny, and Norman promised small classes and individual attention.

Denny didn't want any individual attention, however. Just the opposite: he wanted to blend in and not call attention to himself. In his first nine days at Norman, he had not made any friends, hadn't, in fact, tried to make any. He was a shadow without substance, gliding through his hours in the corridors and classrooms like a ghost, unseen and unheralded. In the classrooms, he tried to sit as far back as possible. He did not volunteer answers.

During lunch, he sat alone in the cafeteria. Actually, there were other guys at the table but he ate quickly, kept his eyes on his plate and faded out of the place as soon as possible. The athletic field was located behind the residence and he made his way there, jogging slightly. Then sat in the bleachers, looking down at the vacant field.

He liked being alone and didn't like it, which was true of his entire life. Being pulled two ways. For instance, he was often lonely and wished for a best friend, above all for a girlfriend. No opportunities for a girlfriend at Norman. He wondered if he really wanted a friend.

He did not want to have happen here what had happened at other places, especially at Bartlett down on the Connecticut border. That had been a beautiful time, for a while. No telephone calls or letters or newspaper stories.

He had played intramural basketball; didn't win any games but didn't goof and lose any, either. He had a small part in a school pageant about the American Revolution, as a minuteman, carrying a musket. Had six lines and remembered them all. Had a best friend, Harvey Snyder, who turned him on to Ed McBain's 87th Precinct novels and the exploits of Steve Carella and Meyer Meyer and the others, more than forty books waiting to be read. Most of all, there was Chloe Epstein. His first sort-of girlfriend. Met her at his first school dance ever. Eighth grade, wore his father's blue and white striped tie, stood uncomfortably against a wall as the DJ spun the records. Girls' choice. Chloe asked him to dance, after crossing the big gym floor toward him. "Don't say no—I'd be so humiliated," she said. Danced, both of them awkward at first, stumbling, then finding a beat, a rhythm, at last. She smelled of peppermint all over. Her cheek touched his and he melted with tenderness. Later they talked, and next day talked again, oh, about everything. Chloe was Jewish, Denny Catholic. He had never met a Jewish person before and she had never really *talked* to a Catholic. They exchanged facts about religion, surprised at all the similarities—Hanukkah and Christmas; bar mitzvah and confirmation; Passover and Easter.

Small and dark and energetic, she was like a hummingbird, going sixty miles an hour while standing still. Eager, talkative, on the move. Let's do this, let's do that. They wrote notes to each other. She signed one: *love.* Which made his heart a dancer, a line from one of his father's old records. All of it wonderful. Until it happened. Damn it.

Shaking off that particular thought, he got up and

headed back to school, taking his time, because his next class was a study period and Mr. Armstrong played it loose with attendance.

At the school steps, he was stopped by Jimmy Burke, one of the few students Denny knew by name. Jimmy was senior class president and had given a "Welcome to Norman" speech at the academy's opening ceremonies. He'd seemed like a nice guy, the right combination of confidence and modesty, as he'd stood on the stage.

"You're Denny Colbert, right?"

Denny nodded, flinching a bit. He wondered whether he had been found out already.

"Listen, we're organizing a new Student Council this year," Jimmy Burke said. "And we're looking for two representatives from each class. Would you be interested?"

"Why me?" Denny asked, genuinely puzzled.

"You're new here. And we need new blood, new ideas."

"I don't know," Denny said. Classic stall. He didn't want to serve on the Student Council at Norman. He had seen a book one day in the Barstow Public Library titled *A Separate Peace*. Later, he had thought: I've declared a separate peace. That's what he wanted to say to Jimmy Burke. But didn't, of course.

Stepping back from Denny and pointing to the residence and the two classroom buildings, Jimmy Burke said: "Everything looks normal at Normal Prep, right?" Shaking his head sadly, he said, "Wrong. This is a great school. No drugs, no guns. But we've still got problems. Guys who want to take over, pushing people around, intimidating young kids. It happens at other schools, too. But it's more damaging here. We're small, only two hundred students. Everything gets magnified . . ."

Denny had not noticed the problems Jimmy Burke talked about. But he hadn't noticed very much, really.

He said, "I've got a lot of studying to do, trying to catch up. I don't think I'd have time for the council."

Jimmy Burke nodded thoughtfully. Then a frown creased his forehead and his eyes lowered. But he looked up immediately, eyes bright again with hope, possibilities. "Look, don't give me a definite answer right now . . . Think about it . . ."

Denny admired guys like Jimmy Burke who passionately believed in a cause, who never took no for an answer.

"Okay," Denny said, knowing his answer would not change.

Later, on the bus going home, he wondered whether he really wanted a separate peace, after all. At Norman Prep, maybe. But not at home. Not with his father, now that the telephone calls had begun.

The opposite of peace was war. Maybe that's what he wanted—a battle against whatever or whoever had thrown a shadow over his family. But, he wondered, how do you start a war?

*H*e entered the apartment to the sound of the telephone splintering the afternoon silence of the rooms. Closing the door behind him, he put down his books and stood in the small foyer, waiting for the phone to stop ringing. Five, six, seven.

Shrugging, he practiced his old method of ignoring the sound, making it a part of the atmosphere, accepting it and going about his usual routine.

In the kitchen, he poured himself a glass of orange juice, spilled a bit on the floor, wiped it up with a paper towel. Twelve, thirteen.

He dug some chocolate chip cookies out of the porcelain jar that said "Coffee." His mother had a strange approach—fourteen, fifteen—to labeling. Her own little codes.

Maybe I should answer it.

He knew the rule.

He stood there with the glass of juice in one hand, the cookie in the other. Did not take a drink, did not take a bite.

Seventeen, eighteen.

He remembered confessing once to a friend, Tommy Cantin, in the seventh grade that he was not allowed to answer the telephone. Tommy had stared at him in disbelief, as if he were a creature from an alien planet. Everybody in America answers the phone, Tommy had said. *Not me,* he had answered. But he was sixteen now—that made a difference.

He went to the bathroom. Closed the door and flushed the toilet, watching the swirling water, the sound obliterating the ringing of the phone. He had used this ploy before.

Emerging from the bathroom, he swore softly—"son of a bitch"—as the phone continued to ring. He had lost count. Must be up to twenty-nine, thirty by now. Still going strong, the sound ominous and threatening.

The record for the afternoon was eighteen rings last year. This was absurd. Thirty-eight? Thirty-nine?

Maybe it was an emergency.

His father injured at work. Or his mother in an accident.

An urgency now in the ringing, filling the rooms, filling his ears, vibrating throughout his body.

He had to stop this crazy ringing.

But he knew the rule. His father's rule: *Do not pick up the phone. Let your mother or me answer it. If it's for you, I will hand it over. Alone in the house, you do not answer.*

Emergency or not, he had to stop the ringing.

More than that: he wanted to start a war, *do* something. Maybe this was a place to begin.

He snatched the phone from its cradle, glad for the sudden absence of ringing, and was astonished to hear his name coming from it.

"Denny . . . Denny . . . is that you?"

He pressed the receiver against his ear.

"Hello . . . hello," the voice said.

He listened, didn't know what to say.

"How are you today, Denny?"

Today? As if they had been speaking yesterday.

"I know you're there, Denny . . ."

A funny voice. Not funny really, but strange, the voice almost familiar, a low smoky kind of voice—a woman? a girl?—intimate, secretive.

"I'd really like to know, Denny: How are you?"

"Fine," he said, having to reply, to say something, but his voice suddenly hoarse.

"Gee . . . that's nice. I'm glad you're fine . . ."

Definitely a woman's voice. Not an old woman but not a girl. Or maybe a girl. He was confused. Confused also because her voice seemed to be mocking him, suggesting that he wasn't fine, not fine at all. Which, at this moment, was true, of course.

Clearing his throat and swallowing hard, he asked: "Who are you?" Blunter than he intended. "I mean—who is this speaking?"

"Somebody," she said. "A friend, maybe. But we don't know each other that well, do we?" Amused now, as if she had said something very amusing. Then: "Yet."

That *yet* hung on the air, like an omen, a black crow on the telephone wires.

"What do you mean, *yet*?" he asked, pouncing on the word. Then realized that he shouldn't be holding this conversation and that he really didn't want to know what she meant.

"I'm sorry," he said. Puzzled about why he should be apologizing. "I have to hang up."

He took the receiver away from his ear, his hand moving in slow motion as in a dream.

"Wait a minute . . . I—" Her voice was amputated as he put down the receiver.

Palms moist, heart thudding, he let himself go limp, as if he had just escaped some terrible fate, like being sucked off a cliff.

He picked up the glass of juice, simply because he had to make some kind of movement. But he didn't drink it, just stood like a statue in the park.

He could hardly believe that he had broken his father's rule.

Denny remembered the day his father had made the rule, a long time ago, so long ago that it was only a dim memory, but one that seized him now with a new immediacy: his father stalking the kitchen, anger like small bolts of lightning in his eyes, then finally standing in front of him like a giant, his legs like stumps of trees.

"Do not ever . . . *ever* . . . answer the telephone again. Understand?"

His father's anger had made tears spring to Denny's

eyes, blinding him. As huge sobs racked Denny's body, his father had enfolded him in his arms, holding him close, all anger gone, all softness and gentleness, murmuring words that soothed him like soft music. Then his mother had joined them, and as the three of them held each other, rocking back and forth, Denny had felt suddenly well loved and protected, despite the phone call and those terrible words . . .

Seven years old. Third grade. Home from school. The house quiet, a stillness that disturbed him, as if someone had turned off the volume of a giant television set. His footsteps echoed on the linoleum as he searched the rooms, calling for his mother. He eventually found her in the bathroom, kneeling on the floor in front of the toilet bowl, limp and moist, her hair damp against her forehead, the smell of vomit in the air.

"Oh, Denny, I'm so sick," she gasped. Then, seeing his anguish at her sickness, "It's just a twenty-four-hour thing. I'll be all right in a while . . ." After which she turned, retching, toward the bowl.

He shut the door softly, at a loss, the thought of his usual after-school lunch of a peanut-butter sandwich repugnant. As he sat in the living room, restless, resisting turning on the television set or even opening a book, not wanting to enjoy himself while his mother was sick in the bathroom, the telephone rang. He hesitated to pick it up. His mother and father always answered the phone. "Let one of us do it," his father always said.

The ringing of the phone emphasized the loneliness of

the house. He realized that he was seldom, if ever, alone at home. His parents were always there. Never had a baby-sitter, even as a child. He counted the rings. One . . . two . . . three . . . Squirmed in the chair, the phone at his elbow. Suppose it was something important. Suppose his father was calling. He strained his ears. Was that a siren he heard in the distance?

The phone continued to ring.

He picked it up.

"Hello," he said, his voice hollow in the room. He had never talked on the phone.

"Who's this?" a voice demanded, a harsh voice, angry. "This isn't the murderer. Who is this? Who's speaking?"

"Me," he answered. Did the voice say *murderer*?

"Who's you?" Impatient, still angry.

"Me, Denny." Then adding his last name: "Colbert."

Pause, then. He looked around, guilty about answering the phone, wishing his mother would come in to take over the call.

"Oh, the murderer's son!"

"You have the wrong number," he said. He had heard about wrong numbers, people making mistakes. *Wrong number* echoed distantly from the past. "There's no murderer here."

"Course there is," the voice said, suddenly not angry anymore, almost gentle. "Your father's John Paul Colbert, isn't he?"

"Yes." Almost stammering that simple word. That simple word that was hard to say all of a sudden.

"Well, if your father is John P. Colbert and you're his

son like you say you are, then you are the son of a murderer. How old are you?"

The question, asked in a return to the angry voice,
caught him off guard. "Seven," he said. "Going on eight."

"Too bad," the voice said. "Too bad to be the son of a
murderer at seven years old."

"My father is not a murderer," he said, shouting into
the phone. "My father is John Paul Colbert and he is not a
murderer."

The telephone was snatched from his hand. He turned
to find his mother standing beside him, all paleness gone,
her face flushed, eyes flashing, her eyes so blazing with—
what?—he did not know what, had never seen it there before. Anger, yes, and something else. She slammed the
phone down on the receiver. Took a deep breath and
swiveled around.

"I'm sorry, Ma," he said, tears springing to his eyes,
turning the world liquid, like he was underwater.

"Hush, hush," she said, her voice funny. "I'm not mad
at you." She clutched him to her. He dove into her, his
face in her skirt, ignoring the terrible smell of vomit that
still clung to her, that obliterated the perfume she always
wore, the smell of flowers in the summer after a rain.

"That man on the phone. He said that Daddy . . ."
He could not say the word, could not get it out.

She thrust him away from her, looked deeply into his
eyes with those deep dark eyes of hers, like the color of
black olives in a jar. "Your father is not a murderer."

"Then why did that man say he was?" he asked.
Surprised by the loss on her face, in her eyes, he sup-

plied his own answer: "Was he joking? Playing a trick on me?"

She smiled, sadly, wanly, a thin smile, a smile without warmth. "There are strange people in the world, Denny. Crazy people who do things that are hard to understand."

And suddenly she was sick again. He saw the sickness in her pallor as if someone had opened a faucet and drained the blood from her face, and she murmured something he did not understand before running off to the bathroom, where he once more heard the terrible sounds of her retching.

Putting his hands over his ears, blotting out the awful sounds, he heard, dimly, the telephone ringing again. He bolted from the room, ran to his bedroom, slammed the door behind him, fell on his knees and crawled under the bed, into the darkness, curling up, arms hugging his knees, eyes closed, glad to be here in the dark where he could not hear the telephone ringing or his mother vomiting.

When his father came home from work, he made the rule:

Never, *never,* answer the phone.

Now, on a September afternoon all these years later, he had broken the rule. The sky hadn't fallen. Lightning hadn't struck. He wondered why he had waited so long.

Suddenly, he was eager for the telephone to ring again. But it didn't.

That night, he awoke to a deafening silence. Checking the digital clock as usual, he saw that it was 3:10, almost the same time as last night's phone call.

The house was quiet—more than quiet: wrapped in an absence of sound so profound that it seemed to be a sound in itself.

But something had awakened him.

Noise in the hallway now, familiar to his ears: a foot-step, a door closing, another footstep. His father, of course.

Denny had never feared a burglar prowling the rooms, because his father often wandered the apartment during the night. Investigating, Denny sometimes found him sitting at a window in the dark or reading a day-old newspaper in the living room, or watching television with the sound turned off.

He wondered now if his father had been waiting for the phone to ring all those nights, had been keeping some kind of rendezvous. He remembered a poem he had read in school during studies about World War I:

I have a rendezvous with death
At some disputed barricade . . .

Was that the kind of rendezvous his father would keep someday, some night?

Stop dramatizing, he told himself.

He slipped out of bed and stood uncertainly in the dark, the linoleum cold under his bare feet. He made his way to the door, feeling his way in the dark, and passed noiselessly through the hallway toward a dim light in the living room.

His father was sitting in his easy chair, not reading, not watching television, just sitting there. Looking at nothing. The expression on his face puzzled Denny. He tried to find a word to describe it. Sad? More than that. Sad and lonesome. Yes, but something else. His eyes lost in thought or memory. Forlorn—that was it, a word that emerged from somewhere, maybe from a book he'd read. Sitting there, forlorn, in the middle of the night. But he and his father and mother were living in a kind of middle of the night even when the sun was shining.

He knew that even if he tried, he could not count how many nights his father had sat up like this, waiting for the call, then answering the telephone. Anger flared within him. His father should retaliate. Hurl the telephone against the wall. Shout at whoever was at the other end of the line. Do *something*. Instead, his father only waited. Meek and mild.

Denny stood there for a while, then finally made his way back to his bedroom, through the long shadows, wondering what his father thought about, sitting up like that, in the middle of the night.

What are you writing about now?

That's Lulu, coming out of nowhere.

I hesitate, cover the page with my hand but know that I can never lie to her.

Aren't you going to tell me?

The Globe, I say. *What happened there.*

Oh.

Sorry, I say. My poor Lulu.

She goes away, leaving scorn behind her like dark weather in the room.

I still dream after all this time of the way she stared at me out of the wreckage, did not really stare because her eyes could not see. Those blank eyes, frozen in her face, and the smear of blood across her cheek.

The rest of her was buried in the wreckage; only the rim of white lace at her throat was visible. Debris covered her body and I felt like I was screaming but couldn't be sure because everything was still, a huge silence surrounding me while I looked down at her in horror.

Then an explosion of sound, screams and cries and someone yelling in my ear, hands pulling and tugging at me, pulling me away. I began to sneeze, once, twice, three times, horrible, dust rising from the rubble, dust clouds blocking out light. My stupid sneezing and my nose running.

My sister, I cried. *She's trapped in there.*

A voice at my ear: *Come on, boy, come on.*

My sister. She might be dead.

I know, I know, but come on, the rest of the balcony could fall. Come on.

Outside, clear sky, faces, sirens screaming, slashes of red fire trucks, white ambulances, everyone running and stumbling, harsh colors bright, hurting my eyes, and I closed them and someone picked me up and rocked me and I smelled smoke and sweat and heard voices:

His sister's dead.

I know.

No pulse, nothing.

Moaning, I opened my eyes, saw other eyes staring down at me, filled with pity. But I didn't want their pity, I wanted my sister back. I didn't want my sister to be dead. Even though I knew it was too late, even for prayers.

* * *

The weeping and the moaning, and what Aunt Mary called the "keening" from the Denehans upstairs, filled the house as if even the walls and ceilings were mourning the dead. Three of the Denehans gone—Eileen and Billy and Kevin—and Mickey in the hospital with a broken pelvis, contusions and abrasions.

Even with her own dead, Mrs. Denehan came down, lines fierce in her face, like gashes, bloodless and deep.

Aunt Mary and Mrs. Denehan wept together, clutching each other while I roamed the rooms, not knowing what to do, where to go, unable to sit or lie down, unable to eat or drink. On the prowl through the rooms, looking for something but not knowing what. I was afraid to close my eyes because I knew what would happen: I would see Lulu's eyes, open and staring and seeing nothing.

The telephone rang, cutting through the moaning. Aunt Mary reached for it, her other arm still embracing Mrs. Denehan and Mrs. Denehan's face like a bruise, all pain.

Aunt Mary listened, her face altering, joy suddenly leaping in her eyes, her mouth open in astonishment. Placing the phone against her thin chest, she announced: *She's alive. Our Lulu's alive . . . at the hospital . . . she's not dead . . .*

In the hospital room, everything white, walls and ceiling as well as the white cast that enclosed Lulu's body like a suit of armor and the bandage around her head like a helmet. Her eyes, dark islands in all that whiteness, looked at us as if from some far distance.

Aunt Mary rushed to her side and I lingered near the doorway. Lulu lay stiff on the bed and did not, maybe could not, lift her arms to receive Aunt Mary.

You're alive, Aunt Mary crooned, *an answer to our prayers, a miracle.*

It wasn't a miracle, Lulu said.

Back from the dead, Aunt Mary said, shaking her head in wonder.

I was not dead, Lulu said, voice sharp and bitter.

Well, whatever, you're with us now, back with us, Aunt Mary said.

I'm not back with you, Lulu said, eyes snapping with anger. *I didn't go anywhere. I'm here. I was always here.*

I finally went to the bed and looked down at her. She closed her eyes and her face closed up, too, shutting us out.

Later, the doctor spoke to us in a small office at the end of the corridor. An old doctor, eyes bloodshot, hair askew, white jacket soiled, reeking of fire and smoke.

Poor you, Aunt Mary murmured. *On the go, all this terrible day.*

I had seen him moving among the injured outside the theater, stethoscope dangling, gnarled hands touching, soothing, passing across bruised flesh.

He sighed, weary, body sagging in the chair. Then: *Let me tell you about Lulu. A remarkable recovery.*

A miracle, Aunt Mary said. *An answer to our prayers.*

Some things are hard to explain, he said, stroking his gaunt face with those old hands. *I'm so tired, so tired. Anyway, we thought we had lost her but she rallied.*

Did her heart stop? I asked, hearing my voice as if someone else had spoken.

It's been a long day, he said, sighing again. Then, briskly: *Let me tell you about her injuries and the prognosis.* He spoke of the fractures and the concussion and the months of therapy and rehabilitation ahead.

He did not say that her heart had stopped.

But did not deny it, either.

Later, I said to Lulu: *Tell me what happened.*

Nothing happened, she said.

When the balcony came down, I told her, *I ducked my head, then found myself on the floor, a seat on top of me. Then I began sneezing, stupid sneezes. What do you remember?*

Nothing, she said.

But her eyes said otherwise. Those snapping black eyes of hers looked away, and Lulu was never one to look away. Especially from me.

Didn't you feel anything, Lulu?

No.

Don't you remember anything?

You're repeating yourself, she said. Then: *I . . . don't . . . remember . . . anything.* Spacing the words. *What more can I say?*

Why are you so mad?

She did not answer, but her anger was like heat coming from a stove.

I knew what I wanted her to say. I wanted her to tell me what happened when her heart stopped beating, when her blood stopped flowing, when the pulse in her temple became perfectly still.

What she saw, what she felt, what it was like to die.

She finally looked me straight in the eye.

I'm not Lazarus, she said.

A long time later, I visited the rehabilitation unit and found her sitting in a chair, bandages removed from her head, wearing a flowered dress Aunt Mary had bought her, the white hospital gown in the closet, at last.

She was studying a folded newspaper in her lap when I came in. She looked up, her face revealing an expression I had never seen there before. My mind scurried to identify it. Anger still there, but more than that. Something calm and cold in her face and eyes, but also deadly.

He went free, she said.

Who?

The boy who started the fire. Who started it all.

She brandished the newspaper, and I saw the picture of the boy, the headline:

USHER CLEARED IN TRAGIC CASE

The boy, she said, *who . . .*

She looked away from me, stared out the window, as if searching the outdoors for something no one else could see. I saw her lips move as she finished the sentence, her voice so low that I couldn't hear the words. Then she turned back to me, a terrible look in her eyes. *The boy who killed me,* she said.

Admitting, at last, that she was Lazarus, after all.

Part Two

*T*his is what Denny's father, John Paul Colbert, thought about in the middle of the night: how his life changed forever at the age of sixteen when he became assistant manager/head usher at the Globe Theater in downtown Wickburg, Massachusetts.

His job was not as glamorous as it sounded. The Globe was a faded relic of Hollywood's golden years, when ornate theaters featured velvet curtains and crystal chandeliers, and snappy ushers in military uniforms guided people to their seats. Those were the days of double features (two movies for the price of one), twelve-chapter cowboy serials at Saturday matinees and Milk Duds for five cents a box. What a time that was!

At least, that's the way Mr. Zarbor described those earlier times. Mr. Zarbor owned the Globe and he liked to tell John Paul about the olden days before television came along and provided free movies at home.

Worst of all, he said, were the shopping centers which later on brought the "cinemas," a word Mr. Zarbor detested. "Cinema One and Two," he lamented. "Made of cinder blocks. No velvet curtain—no curtains at all."

The Globe featured foreign movies that never made it to the shopping centers, and provided a place in downtown Wickburg for special programs like the annual Christmas show, when the *Nutcracker Suite* was presented for young and old alike, and appearances by old-time big bands. Mr. Zarbor loved variety acts—magicians, tap dancers, jugglers and acrobats. He was most proud of his annual "Monster Magic Show" each Halloween, a program for the city's children, especially orphans and those in foster homes. Although the Wickburg Rotary Club was the official sponsor, John Paul's father told him that Mr. Zarbor paid most of the acts out of his own pocket.

John Paul worked at the theater weekends and two or three nights a week, depending on business. He sold tickets at the box office, swept the floors, ran errands. Mr. Zarbor was a good boss. He sympathized with John Paul and his family. They had arrived from Canada a few years before to start a new life in the United States. Mr. Zarbor had been an immigrant whose family had fled Hungary a generation earlier, when he was sixteen years old, exactly John Paul's age. "You remind me of myself," Mr. Zarbor said.

In the United States, John Paul woke up every day with great expectations. His parents had been eager to leave the small parish north of Montreal in the Province of Quebec. His father, a quick-talking impatient man, claimed that the French-speaking people of Quebec were treated as second-class citizens by the Canadian government. He and John Paul's mother spent their savings on their son's education, sending him to a private school in Montreal where classes focused on the English language and U.S. culture and history. When he and his parents moved south, John Paul was ready, although he had certain doubts. Language, for one thing. He spoke without a heavy accent but his English was stilted and formal, learned from books and not from conversation. At Wickburg Regional High School, he was glad to lose himself among hundreds of other students while he adjusted to his new life.

John Paul's parents adjusted quickly to life in Wickburg. His father found a job immediately as a chef in a French restaurant downtown, and dreamed of the day when he would open his own place. His mother kept busy with the activities of St. Therese's Church. She sold cards at the Friday night beano parties and visited the sick and the shut-ins.

The restaurant where John Paul's father worked was next to the Globe Theater. He struck up an acquaintance with Mr. Zarbor—they both loved foreign movies, especially French and Italian films—and this led to John Paul's employment at the theater.

Life, John Paul reflected, was good. As far as language was concerned, he would have to learn contractions. That was his biggest difficulty. Mr. Burns, his English teacher, said: "Your vocabulary is excellent but you have to learn to say *don't* or *aren't* or *doesn't*. Instead of *do not, are not* or *does not.*"

"I will try," John Paul said. In his mind he used contractions, but when he spoke, they disappeared.

"No—*I'll try*," the teacher said, kind but firm. "That's the only way you'll sound like a real U.S. teenager."

"Okay," John Paul said. *Okay*—a safe American word that always came in handy.

Preparations for the magic show began early that year, featuring "Martini the Magnificent," a magician who often appeared on children's television programs. His performance included sawing a woman not only in half, but in five separate pieces, sudden disappearances and strange rituals featuring ghosts and goblins. His act also called for special constructions backstage, where John Paul learned to his disappointment that there was no magic at all in Martini's act. All of it was mechanical, not mystical. It was like learning that there was no Santa Claus—a wonderful moment of discovery followed by the bleak lonesome truth. Martini himself, when he showed up, turned out to be a fussy, demanding man whose real name was unromantic and ordinary: Oscar Jones.

Preparing for the big day, John Paul vacuumed the faded carpet in the aisles, tried to scrape away the remains of chewing gum from the cement floor under the seats, did his best to repair seats that did not fold down properly. Mr. Zarbor paid him time and a half for overtime and treated him to sundaes and ice cream sodas after the work was done for the day.

"What about the balcony?" John Paul asked. He had heard that the balcony, closed for many years, might be reopened for Martini because a bigger audience than usual was expected.

They both looked up at the cluttered, forbidding balcony, long used as a place for storage.

Mr. Zarbor sighed hugely. "Forget it, the balcony," he said. "It would take an army to move all that stuff. We'll arrange for an extra performance if it becomes necessary . . ."

"Okay," John Paul replied cheerfully. He avoided the balcony if possible. When he was sent there, he often heard rats scurrying among the debris and strange crackling sounds. He always looked around nervously, expecting . . . he did not know what he expected. We should clean the balcony up, he thought. But he never said anything to Mr. Zarbor. Too big a job, removing all that junk.

John Paul awakened early the day of the magic show, glad that Halloween this year fell on a Saturday because that added to the drama of the event. He looked forward to seeing the show through the innocent eyes of the children, hoping this would bring back some of the magic that had disappeared when he'd seen the backstage facts.

On the way to the Globe early that afternoon, he was hurried along by brisk howling winds that shook leaves from their branches, creating a snowfall of many colors.

Low clouds were heavy with rain that maybe would come later. Perfect weather for Halloween and a mysterious magic show.

When he arrived at the theater, Mr. Zarbor was talking to the six high-school kids he had hired to help out that afternoon. Although they were students at Wickburg Regional, John Paul did not recognize any of them. Four boys and two girls. His eyes were immediately drawn to a slender, blond girl whose hair flowed to her shoulders. Her eyes were a deep dark brown, in sharp contrast to her hair. A pang pierced his heart. He was always drawn to impossible loves, those always out of reach: movie stars, cheerleaders at football games, lovely girls walking down the street.

"Ah, you're here," Mr. Zarbor said, spotting John Paul. Then to the high schoolers, "This is your boss. He will be in charge for the afternoon. John Paul Colbert."

Blushing furiously, John Paul faced his small audience. He tried to avoid looking at the beautiful blonde, afraid he would not be able to speak at all. The four boys were tall and gangly, probably basketball players. The other girl was small and dark-haired and seemed nervous, clearing her throat, tiny hands touching her cheeks, her nose, her hair.

Mr. Zarbor had rehearsed the instructions with him. They were simple assignments, thank goodness.

Taking a deep breath, he told the four boys that they were assigned to general duties: watching the children, helping them find seats (some were only five or six years old), keeping an eye out for older troublemakers. He realized he was making a speech. He told himself to watch his contractions.

"Don't scold the young children," he said, conscious that he had avoided *do not*. "They will be excited but will settle down after a while." He had missed *they'll*, had used *they will*.

Turning to the girls, he was crushed to find the beautiful one stifling a yawn. The other girl stared at him intently, frowning. He concentrated on her. The girls would be in charge of the candy counter before the show started. Candy and popcorn were free but the children needed coupons to obtain them. Later, the girls would patrol the aisles with the boys, making sure the children were safe, looking for children who might have become sick. Who knows?

The boys asked a few simple questions. He answered them without wasting words, watching his contractions.

Ten minutes later, and forty-five minutes before curtain time, the children arrived in six big orange buses. They marched into the theater in orderly fashion, as if taking part in a parade. Boys with ties, hair neatly combed. Girls in dresses. Mostly young children, the oldest eleven or twelve. All of them trying to suppress their excitement but suddenly breaking ranks, whooping and yelling with sheer delight. "They go crazy at first but they settle down after a while," Mr. Zarbor had told him.

The hired boys did their best to guide the children to their seats and to maintain some kind of order. But order was not the order of the day. The children ran all over the place, rushing for the front rows, climbing over seats, saving places for friends, pushing and shoving, all in great good spirits. In the lobby, the two high-school girls worked frantically as the children stormed the candy counter as if it were a fort to be taken.

John Paul was here, there and everywhere. Answering questions, giving directions to the rest rooms. Called to the candy counter to settle an argument: Some children had not been issued coupons or had forgotten to bring them. Others had five or six. The rule had been two coupons per child, don't spend them both at once. The girls looked at him desperately. "Only fifteen minutes to go," he consoled them. The lights blinked, once, twice, three times. He was wrong. "Ten minutes to go," he told the girls. Mr. Zarbor had allowed ten minutes for the children to settle down. Which they did quickly, finding their seats, speaking in whispers, although a few could not resist throwing popcorn around.

"Always a mistake, the popcorn," Mr. Zarbor told John Paul as they stood down front near the stage. "A big cleanup job. But what's a show without popcorn?"

Glancing at his watch, Mr. Zarbor said: "Five minutes more. Then the big bang . . ."

John Paul knew what Mr. Zarbor meant. Martini the Magnificent was especially proud of his dramatic opening. First a big boom, like an explosion, which never failed, he said, to bring on a stunning silence. Then total darkness. So dark the audience would not see the curtain silently part and open. Then a small dim light onstage, followed by another. Then another. Pinpoints of light like tiny stars winking in a darkened sky. Finally, Martini would appear as if suspended in the darkness. And the show would commence.

A mysterious and magic moment occurs a few minutes before a stage show begins, as if a silent signal has been sent. John Paul had seen this happen a number of times. It was happening now. The theater became quiet, a spooky kind of quiet. There was no clock in the theater and most of the children did not have watches, but they sensed that the show was about to start. They were instantly subdued, as if every child in the place had taken a deep breath and was holding it.

Awed by the stillness, John Paul was startled when Mr. Zarbor touched his arm. "What was that?" Mr. Zarbor asked. His voice a whisper in the quietness.

John Paul frowned. Did he mean the sudden absence of sound? No, something else. "Listen." Now John Paul heard something. But what? A slow creaking sound. He thought, for some reason, of a ship tearing loose from its mooring, its deck creaking eerily, although he had never heard such a sound before—unless he'd heard it in a movie.

The sound again. Louder.

He and Mr. Zarbor exchanged puzzled looks.

The noise: this time like a huge nail being pulled from a board by a hammer. Crazy, but that is what it sounded like to him. A creaking, yanking noise. From the balcony.

John Paul looked, and so did Mr. Zarbor. John Paul thought some kids might have crept up there and were fooling around in the junk and debris.

"Better go see," Mr. Zarbor said.

Dark up there, as usual. "I do not have my flashlight," John Paul said.

"Here." Mr. Zarbor handed him a book of matches.

Reluctantly, John Paul made his way up the center

aisle and through the lobby, then ascended the soiled carpeted steps to the balcony. The giant chandelier hanging from the ceiling gave no light: the bulbs had long ago burned out. He squinted into the semidarkness at the accumulation of junk. Old newspapers, cartons, piles of rags, old rolled-up posters. Saw no one. Was startled by that strange creaking sound almost beneath his feet. Much louder than before.

Then: the explosion from the stage as the show began, the sound booming through the air, banging against the walls, echoing from the high ceiling. The delighted cries and gasps of the children. Then darkness. And silence.

John Paul blinked: like being struck blind, this utter darkness.

A movement beneath his feet as if he were standing on a ship that was leaving the dock.

He struck a match, missed the first time, tried again. The flame created a small bright cave in the darkness. Suddenly the entire matchbook caught fire, because he had held the flaming match too close to the others. Pain singed his palm. He dropped the matchbook, watched it flare toward the floor and, to his horror, saw it ignite a ribbon of crepe paper draped over a cardboard box.

He tried to stamp out the flame but was thrown off-balance as the floor swayed beneath his feet.

"Fire!" someone yelled from the stage. Someone who saw the flames and knew this was not part of the show's opening. The floor lurched again, definite this time. The impossible thought, *earthquake,* came to his mind.

"Fire!" The voice now a scream filled with terror.

The audience did not respond, while all the time the

flames were spreading to a pile of newspapers and another cardboard box. Smoke erupted, rolling between the seats.

"Fire!" This time, no doubt at all. The sheer terror in that voice began a stirring down below. John Paul, in panic, advanced a foot or two but the floor shifted violently under his feet, rumbling, crackling, sending him reeling, his arms flailing helplessly.

He tried desperately to regain his balance, smelled the stench of smoke and heard the screams of children. Standing almost on tiptoe, perched like a bird about to take flight, he felt the floor, with a terrible shudder, give way beneath his feet.

*H*e did not wake up all at once but drifted in and out of consciousness. All he remembered later was a rising and falling, a reaching up toward lights that blinded his eyes and plunging down again into darkness. Then, voices, mumbling words he could not understand. Different voices, sharp and loud then soft and murmuring, his mother's voice once, speaking in French. Then down again into a darkness that was sweet and safe.

Next came the pain. His head throbbed with the pain, pulsed with it, as if he were wearing a steel helmet that was too small for his head, too tight, threatening to crush his skull. His skull a mass of pain.

Sometimes the pain receded and went away, and he would drift lazily, carried on gentle waves. When he'd try to move with the waves, he'd find himself paralyzed, trapped, his arms pinned down. He was aware of being connected to something. *Connected,* as if he were part of some terrible machinery. That's when the panic began, screaming inside him. Until the darkness came. Or maybe the pain. Even the pain was better than the panic.

At some point he began to dream. Visions filled the darkness, shoutings filled his ears. He was being chased, pursued, tracked down. Shadows behind him, footsteps coming closer, closer. Children shouting and crying. Something terrible chasing him, pursuing him, coming closer while all the time the children cried . . .

. . . Until he opened his eyes, blinking against the brightness of daylight slashing at his eyeballs. He quickly closed them again, seeking the comfort and safety of the dark.

Next time he woke up, he found his mother and father looking down at him as if from a great distance, their eyes wide with concern and worry. They seemed to be looking at him through a microscope as he lay pinned down on some Biology I glass slide.

He knew instantly that he was in a hospital bed and that the helmet on his head was not a helmet at all but bandages. His arm was connected to a nearby monitor that beeped and hummed. Another tube was connected to an upside-down bottle suspended in the air. His head did not hurt much at the moment. There was only a dull ache. But his eyes still stung from the brightness.

His mother's eyes were wet with tears. She kept saying his name over and over. *"Jean-Paul . . . Jean-*

Paul . . ." In the French way. She used to croon him to sleep murmuring his name. But such sorrow in her voice now. He had never heard such sorrow in her voice.

He wanted to reassure her. *I am fine, Mama, I am fine.* But he was not certain if he was fine or not, and the pressure on his skull became intense and began to brighten with pain.

"Take it easy, John Paul," his father said, speaking in English tinged with the old Canadian accent. "Easy, easy . . ." He never spoke French anymore.

"Am I okay?" he asked, his voice surprisingly thin. He felt the panic beginning again, a shivering in his spine because they were looking at him seriously, as if they did not recognize him as their son. "Am I going to die?"

"Non . . . non . . . non . . . ," his mother whispered, shaking her head vigorously and bending to kiss him wetly on the cheek.

"You were hurt," his father said. "A concussion—serious, yes, but a fracture, no. Enough to put you out for a few days."

"How long?" John Paul asked. "How many days?"

His father lifted his shoulders, grimaced, as if reluctant to answer. "Six days—but you are back with us now. That is all that counts."

"That is all?"

But that was not all, because suddenly everything that had happened came back to him, and he heard again the crackle of flames, saw that snake of fire uncoiling at his feet and, God, the balcony coming apart under his feet and then, the smoke and flames and the screaming children below—loud, then faint, fainter.

He drifted mercifully into the sweet safety of the dark again.

The next time he opened his eyes his parents were gone. He was flat on his back looking up at the ceiling, which had a swirling pattern, like waves frozen in an arctic ocean. He moved his head tentatively and was relieved to find that his bad headache had disappeared. Only the strange pressure remained. He heard the low murmur of the monitor close by and raised himself on one elbow to look at it.

A man sitting in a chair by the window rose to his feet and approached the bed. The man was about his father's age but taller, with massive shoulders and a craggy face with deep lines etched into the flesh like Mr. Zarbor. His eyes focused on John Paul as if trying to read his mind, as if, in fact, he *could* read his mind.

"How are you, John Paul?" he asked, his voice as gentle as his eyes were sharp.

John Paul was suddenly afraid to speak.

"Do you feel well enough to answer some questions?"

Still kindly, still gentle, but John Paul tensed, making his arms and legs rigid, holding his body in check. He became aware of his heart beating, like a caged thing in his ribs. Before he could answer, the man said: "My name is Adam Polansky. I am the public safety commissioner for the city of Wickburg. I have been placed in charge of the investigation of the tragic events at the Globe Theater." He spoke formally, as if complying with some rule about properly announcing his name and purpose. Then gently again: "I'd appreciate anything you can tell me about what happened that day."

John Paul was afraid to speak. As if he had something to hide, something to be ashamed of.

"I know this is difficult for you but it's very important for our investigation . . ."

That word again. *Investigation.* Maybe that's what had touched off the fear of answering. And the guilt. He didn't know why he should feel any guilt.

"Did I do something wrong?" he asked.

"It's not a question of right or wrong, John Paul. It's a question of getting at the truth of the situation," Adam Polansky said. "You can help us . . ."

A movement near the door caught John Paul's attention. Turning his head tentatively, he saw another man, tall and thin—thin lips, thin nose—wearing a hat with a visor pulled down over his eyes. He had been standing silently near the door but came forward now, as if he had just swallowed something bitter and foul-tasting. More than sour: his eyes below the visor looked at John Paul suspiciously.

"You're too soft, Commissioner," the man said to Adam Polansky but still looking at John Paul.

"Take it easy, Cutter," the commissioner said. "He's just a kid." Then to John Paul: "This is Detective Lawrence Cutter. With the Wickburg police . . ."

"Here," the detective said, thrusting the newspaper at John Paul.

The headlines, blunt in huge black type, streamed across the top of the front page:

22 CHILDREN DIE IN THEATER DISASTER

A smaller headline underneath:

BALCONY COLLAPSE, FIRE UNDER PROBE

A third headline in slightly smaller type:

USHER, 16, TO BE QUESTIONED

Stephen Delaney, 9.

Nancy Saladora, 6.

Kevin Thatcher, 13.

Deborah Harper, 5.

Suzanne Henault, 10.

He dropped the newspaper on the bed and closed his eyes to shut away the names, but they blazed in his mind, pulsing like neon.

Richard O'Brien, 11.

Stephanie Albertson, 9.

Arthur Campbell, 7.

Before he'd read the names in stark black type, the fact of twenty-two children dead at the Globe Theater here in Wickburg had refused to register in his mind. Tragedies like that happened in other places, faraway places. 300 DEAD

IN A PLANE CRASH IN CHICAGO. L.A. FIRE CLAIMS 50 LIVES. Headlines he remembered. But 22 DIE IN WICKBURG? Impossible.

Then the names.

Lucy Amareault, 10.

Daniel Kelly, 7.

James Bickley, 6.

And he remembered the faces. Was Lucy Amareault, 10, the small girl in the bright red dress, two teeth missing in front, who spilled chocolate ice cream all over herself? Or was Lucy the older girl, in charge of two small boys, acting like a grown-up mother, telling the boys to "stand up straight and behave yourselves"? Did one of those possible Lucys lie crushed and broken under the balcony a few minutes later? He twisted in the bed, trying to turn from the thought, but his mind refused to obey. Because—what about James Bickley, 6? Was he the boy with hair the color of a Sunkist orange who hadn't quite made it to the rest room and stood in the lobby, crying, inconsolable, as a wet blotch appeared on the front of his pants?

Another terrible question that he could not avoid:

Am I to blame?

He was not sure whether he had spoken aloud. He clung to the words Commissioner Polansky had spoken after Detective Cutter had brandished the newspaper: "You are not being charged with anything, John Paul."

John Paul had looked immediately at the detective, but did not see any mercy or gentleness in those hard eyes.

At that moment, the questioning had been interrupted

by Ellie, a kindly nurse, who said that it was time for John Paul's treatment. Winking at John Paul, rescuing him from the clutches of the investigators. "We'll be back," Detective Cutter promised as he placed the newspaper on the bed, his words like a threat lingering in the air.

Now John Paul returned to the newspaper, forcing himself to read again the story of the balcony's collapse— the fire, the smoke, the panic, the heroic efforts to rescue the children, the words at times having no meaning, as if his mind refused to translate the nightmarish parade of letters into actual words.

His own name leaped from the page:

> John Paul Colbert, 16, a part-time employee, was dispatched to the balcony to investigate what Zarbor called "strange sounds" about five minutes prior to the start of the show. Moments later, flames erupted in the balcony, and at the cry of "fire" pandemonium reigned. As the flames gathered in intensity, the balcony gave way, crashing down on the unsuspecting children below.
>
> Fire authorities are investigating the possible connection between the fire and the balcony's collapse. Colbert, who is recovering from head injuries suffered when he was pulled down into the wreckage, is scheduled to be questioned as soon as his condition allows. He is reported in stable condition at Wickburg General Hospital.

What about Mr. Zarbor? he wondered.

He searched the story and found the following paragraphs:

Zarbor, who had owned and operated the theater for 32 years, was reported in a state of shock and
was treated by his family physician.

City Building Inspector Cyril Chatham said he
had cited the theater owner for several violations of
the municipal codes during an official inspection in
August. The balcony was a special concern of his report and he ordered Zarbor to have construction ex-
perts inspect it within 90 days. Zarbor, apparently,
ignored the order. The 90-day period ended the day
before the tragedy.

John Paul reassembled the newspaper, inserting pages
that had fallen aside, folding it neatly, absently, his hands
working independently of his mind, his mind having itself
become a haunted theater where the balcony crashed again
and again, crushing the children below.

Why *had* the balcony collapsed?

Too old, too loaded with junk, he told himself.

Did the fire weaken the floor, causing whatever sup-
ported the balcony to break loose?

Was the fire to blame?

Look who started the fire.

Me, he cried silently.

Me. Me. Me. Me.

Nighttime. Stillness pervaded in the room. No hum
or beeping of the monitor. The padding of rubber soles
in the corridors as the nurses glided to and from the
rooms. Venetian blinds shuttered against the outside darkness.

Television voices, muted and distant, in the air, his own set suspended high in a corner of the room, like a huge blind cyclops. The monotonous voice on the intercom summoning doctors. *Dr. Conroy . . . Dr. Tibbets . . . call Central . . .* Moments of sudden silence in which he could hear the soft *ding* as the elevator doors out in the corridor opened and closed.

He had dozed fitfully, dipping beneath the surface and then rising suddenly, aware of dreams but unable to recall them, only the mood, the aura, the mood black, the aura sad and dismal. All that he could remember of the dreams was the rain falling, falling everywhere, and suddenly turning to silver and then red and then from red to blood.

Emerging from yet another half-shaped dream, vestiges of sleep tugging at his eyelids, he saw an apparition at the doorway. A ghost. No, not a ghost, as he half-raised himself, squinting, but a woman in a gray raincoat, long gray hair framing her gray face, her eyes not gray but fiercely black, burning out at him, as if something behind her eyes had caught fire.

She lifted her right hand and pointed a long withering finger at him.

"You!"

He had never heard such hate and loathing in a single syllable. Then again:

"You." Vomiting the word.

Slowly advancing into the room, her feet dragging as if she were slogging through water, she screamed: "Murderer . . ." Voice raspy, hoarse. The finger pointing accusingly, her face taut, terrible.

"You killed my Joey!"

He closed his eyes, as if by doing so he could rid himself of this apparition, this wretched figure from a nightmare world. Eyes tightly closed, which instantly brought on a headache, the painful tightening of his skull. Through the pain he heard other voices and rushing feet, and opened his eyes to see the woman struggling in the arms of nurses, pinning her down, the woman moaning, awful sounds coming from her, lamenting, sobbing, eyes still wild like pain made visible. Twisting and writhing, she was taken from the room, half-carried, half-dragged until, at the door, she sagged in the arms of a huge nurse and allowed herself to be taken away, wailing miserably.

Later, Ellie came in, bringing a basin and towel, to bathe his face. She was younger than his mother, but her hair was completely white.

Before he could ask her anything, she said: "Don't let that upset you, John Paul. Poor woman. Her son died at the Globe. She can't cope." While she caressed his cheeks, his neck, his forehead with the damp warm cloth.

"But she thinks that I—"

"Hush, hush," Ellie said. "You did nothing. But she's lost all sense of reality. Relax, now. Float. I'll give you a pill to let you sleep."

But I did something wrong.

The matches.

The fire.

In the confusion of waking suddenly and the woman's invading the room, he had forgotten the fire and how he had started it.

He doubted he would sleep again even if the nurse gave him a pill.

*　　*　　*

The next day, the truth was made plain. A gathering in his room: his mother and father, arms around each other near the window, Commissioner Polansky and Cutter, the sharp-voiced man, near his bed. He listened as they spoke, nodding, understanding, head clear, pain gone, but a terrible heaviness in his chest—not his chest but his heart or whatever place or space inside of him where guilt or loneliness became real. Anyway, he listened. He did not mention that small space to anyone.

He nodded, clinging to the words of the commissioner: he was not responsible for the tragedy. Yes, it had been unwise of him to light that match in the dark, in that cluttered balcony, but the fire had had nothing to do with the collapse of the balcony. In fact, the flames had sent a warning, an alarm that something was wrong in the theater, causing some children to flee immediately, probably saving their lives. "You were not to blame," Adam Polansky said. "But . . ."

But. That dangerous, sly word, slinking into the conversation like a tiny snake of accusation.

"But somebody was to blame for the collapse," Detective Cutter interrupted. "And this is where you come in. Where you must tell the truth."

For some reason, John Paul thought of Mr. Zarbor. Poor Mr. Zarbor. Was he still in that state of shock the newspapers mentioned?

"Mr. Zarbor . . . ," he said.

"Exactly," the detective said. "You must not protect

anyone. Mr. Zarbor or anyone else. You must tell the truth, not hide anything."

But he wasn't hiding anything.

Detective Cutter spoke again: "Did Mr. Zarbor ever mention the condition of the balcony to you?"

"No. I put things up there. Boxes, stuff from backstage. I did not go up there when I didn't have to. I did not like the balcony."

"Why not?"

"It was spooky, dark. Sometimes I heard noises—like rats running around . . ."

"Are you sure it was rats?"

"I thought it was." His headache was returning with a bang, like a nail being driven into his head.

"Could the sound have been something else?"

"Like what?"

"Like the sound you heard just before the balcony collapsed. There's reason to believe that the balcony had begun a slow collapse before the day of the show. Did Mr. Zarbor ever mention the condition of the balcony before that day?"

Hadn't he asked that question a minute ago?

"No." A hammer was pounding the nail home, high at the back of his skull.

At that moment, his father intervened.

"I think my son's in pain," he said. "Enough."

The detective stepped back toward the doorway and the commissioner came to John Paul's bedside. "Try to get some rest," he said, kindly, gently.

"But think about those questions," Detective Cutter

called over his shoulder as he left the room. His voice was not kind or gentle.

The next morning, a small man, so short he was barely visible over the wagon he pushed, paused at the doorway and asked John Paul if he wanted to buy any candy or gum, magazines or newspapers.

"If you've got no money pay me later," he called cheerfully.

"Can I buy a newspaper?" John Paul asked, immediately regretting it. He did not really want to read more newspaper stories about the Globe. "My father left money in the drawer." Nodding toward the bureau next to the bed.

"My name's Mac," the man said. "I'm three feet nine and used to be in the circus. What a juggler! I used to perform at the Globe. Before your time. How old do you think I am?"

All of this while he brought over the newspaper, took the money from the drawer, deposited change in the drawer and handed the newspaper to John Paul.

"I don't know," John Paul said, glad for his company, for someone in his room who was not a doctor or nurse or investigator.

"Fifty-one. Everybody says I don't look a day over thirty." Shaking his head: "Too bad about Mr. Zarbor. He was a nice man. Had a soft spot for jugglers . . ."

Too bad? Was a nice man? Danger in those words. John Paul snatched the newspaper from Mac's hands, moaned as he saw the headline:

THEATER OWNER COMMITS SUICIDE;
DESPONDENT OVER PENDING CHARGES

That night, he prayed for the soul of Mr. Zarbor and for all the children who died in the theater. He said a rosary, counting off the prayers on his fingers. Then another rosary and another, hundreds of *Notre Pères* and *Ave Marias*—he always said his prayers in French—until he slipped, finally, into sleep. Sleep which had somehow become a sweet and cherished friend.

Three days later, he was discharged from the hospital. His mother and father came to take him home. They fussed over him. His mother helped him dress, although he felt capable of dressing himself. She knelt to lace his shoes, which embarrassed him. His father kept touching him— his shoulder, his hair—as if to verify John Paul's existence.

Finally, Ellie, the white-haired nurse, came with a wheelchair. "Hop in," she said. "You're getting a free ride."

John Paul resisted. "I can walk," he said. "I feel fine . . ."

"A rule of the hospital," Ellie said, leading him to the wheelchair. "Everybody gets a ride to the front door."

But as they began their journey down the corridor, they headed away from the bank of elevators leading to the first floor and the main entrance.

"Where are we going?" he asked.

He saw the uncertainty on his parents' faces, saw Ellie's grim determination. "We're going down the service elevator. To the back of the hospital. It'll be quicker this way."

"Why quicker?" he asked, suddenly alert, realizing that his parents had been more than concerned this morning. They'd been worried, tense, touching him, dressing him to cover their nervousness.

Nobody spoke.

The elevator doors opened, and they entered. They descended in silence. John Paul didn't ask any more questions. He didn't want to know the answers. He thought he knew, however, why they were avoiding the front of the hospital. He remembered the woman who had yelled accusations at him a few nights ago. Maybe she was waiting for him in the front of the building, with others like herself who blamed him for what happened at the theater.

The doors opened smoothly, silently. John Paul saw a police officer standing at the rear exit of the hospital. He beckoned to them, an old cop with a ruddy complexion, a grandfatherly kind of man. "The taxi is waiting," he said. "Hurry, before they find out what's happening."

John Paul was wheeled to the doorway. His father helped him up from the wheelchair, although he needed no help. Ellie kissed him briefly on the cheek. "God be with you," she said. "Poor boy . . ."

Through the doors and across the sidewalk and into the opened door of the taxi, his mother and father hurrying him inside. The taxi smelled of cigarette smoke. The driver, hunched over the wheel, did not look at them. "Hold on," he muttered as the taxi shot away with squealing tires, bursts of foul exhaust obliterating the smell of smoke.

As they turned the corner leading away from the hospital, John Paul looked out the rear window. A small crowd had gathered at the hospital's front entrance, holding up signs and placards, like pickets at the scene of a strike. He could not read the crudely scrawled words from this distance. As he watched, the crowd began to scatter across the lawn, heading for the rear entrance which the taxi had left only moments before. They halted in their tracks, as if realizing they had been tricked. John Paul saw fists raised in anger, faces raw with rage.

"They think I'm guilty," he said, knowing that the anger and rage were for him.

"You are not," his mother said, pulling him to her.

But I must be, he thought miserably, as the taxi roared through the streets toward home.

*I*n the next few days, John Paul wondered whether he had come home too soon. He was not sure. He had been eager to leave the hospital, to have his bandages removed, to get away from the deadly routine of blood tests, blood pressure readings and a thermometer stuck under his tongue three or four times a day. The food always looked delicious on the plate but was tasteless in his mouth. The open door to his room had made him nervous, especially after that woman had invaded it, yelling accusations at him.

But, once at home, he was restless, roaming the rooms like an alien in a place that had always been safe. Not that he had ever felt danger anywhere, either at home or on the streets or at Wickburg Regional. A different kind of safety was now involved. He groped for the word, searching through his English and French vocabulary, and found it at last—"security," although he pronounced it aloud the

French way: *"sécurité."* With the proper accents in place in his mind.

But no *sécurité* now. Even with his father sleeping away the morning—he still worked nights at the restaurant—and his mother busy with housework, he did not feel at ease. His headaches had stopped, his cuts and bruises healed. But he wondered whether something had happened to his mind that could not be cured. Something more than his mind, however. Something else entirely. Which he did not want to think about.

He told his mother: "I am going for a walk."

She put down the big spoon with which she was stirring something in a pan on the stove. "Should you do that?"

"I will be going to school next week. Why not a walk this week? You told me I am pale. Maybe fresh air will help." He did not use contractions with his mother.

She nodded, eyes sad. Since the tragedy, she wore sadness like a coat she could not take off.

The coldness of November greeted him as he stepped out of the house, and he raised the collar of his jacket. The sky, dark and low, pressed down upon him. Tree branches, stark and leafless, were like spiderwebs climbing against the grayness of the sky. Chilled and depressed, watching pieces of debris kicked across the sidewalk by a brisk wind, he almost went back into the house.

He headed for the Wickburg Memorial Library. Did not know he had left the house for this purpose until this moment, yet had known all along that he *had* to go, had to find out what had happened outside the hospital while he was a patient there.

Luckily, he did not have to spend time learning how to use the microfilm equipment. A cheerful librarian told him that the most recent newspapers had not yet been filmed, and she brought him all the newspapers for the past two weeks, placing them on a table in the reading room. She did not question why he was not in school.

An hour later, he stumbled out of the library. The headlines and stories raced through his mind as he made his way on wobbly legs up Main Street. He paused at a mailbox, leaning against it, his breath coming rapidly, dangerously, as if he had been running at a furious pace.

Lifting his face to the wind, he was grateful for having been in the hospital immediately after the tragedy, for having been spared the agony of those terrible days of rage and pain. Black headlines and story after story told of children trapped, children hurt, children dead. Pictures had been supplied by grieving families: first communions, school photos, family gatherings. Eager faces, shining eyes. A boy on Santa's lap. A girl blowing out candles on a birthday cake. And there were pictures of funerals, too, of crowds outside churches, faces twisted with grief, eyes drowning with tears.

Then a shocking picture of himself, surrounded by happy children, all beaming at the camera, taken, apparently, in the lobby of the theater. He did not remember posing for the picture. He read the sentence under the photo: "Usher John Paul Colbert shown with children shortly before tragedy struck at the Globe Theater. Colbert

82

has been cleared of responsibility for the collapse of the balcony."

As he made his way home, that was his one shred of comfort. *Cleared of responsibility.*

But a very small and slender shred.

All those children had died.

And he had been a part of it.

A letter awaited him at home. His mother looked at him expectantly as she handed it over: he had never received a letter before. On his birthday, his mother and father always sent him a card in the mail, timing it to arrive on the correct date. But this was a *letter,* a long white envelope, delicate handwriting spelling out his name and address.

He weighed it in the palm of his hand, reluctant to open it.

He couldn't imagine who could be writing to him.

He looked for the return address—none.

As he tore the envelope open carefully at one end, his father emerged from the bedroom, yawning, running his hand through sleep-rumpled hair.

"A letter for John Paul," his mother announced to him, apprehension in her voice.

His parents watched as he withdrew a sheet of paper from the envelope. More delicate handwriting, and a faint whiff of perfume. A bouquet of blue flowers decorated the top right corner of the letter. An address in Wickburg took up the other corner.

Tilting the letter to the light from the window, he read the following:

Dear John Paul,

You may not remember me. My name is Nina Citrone. I was one of the high-school kids Mr. Zarbor hired to help out the day of the magic show.

I am writing to tell you how sorry I am about what happened. I know that you must be feeling unhappy. I read about your injuries and hope that you are feeling better. Thank God I escaped without getting hurt.

You were very kind to me the day of the show. I was nervous and you went out of your way to make me feel at ease.

I hope you are recovering on schedule and will be back in school soon.

Wasn't that a terrible day? I still have nightmares. I see the crashing of the balcony just before I wake up. I pray for the souls of those poor children every night when I say my prayers.

Thank you again for being so nice to me.

Sincerely,
Nina Citrone

He handed the letter to his mother and went to the window and looked out at the street. He did not want to look at his mother because he would have to confess that he could not recall being kind to Nina Citrone. He himself had been nervous that day, had tried to be helpful to everyone, answering questions, giving directions, trying to appear calm in all the turmoil. He had been attracted to the blond girl, not the nervous one who could not stand still, always moving her hands, shuffling her feet.

"A nice letter, that," his father said, looking over his wife's shoulder. "We are proud of you, John Paul . . ."

"You must answer her," his mother said. *"Demain."* Then, catching herself: "Tomorrow."

Maybe the letter was an omen of good things coming at last, he thought that night as he prepared for bed.

Let me count the good things for a change, he thought, kneeling to say his prayers. I have not had a headache for three days. I will be going back to school on Monday. My name has been cleared, even though there were no big headlines announcing it. And a girl has written me a letter.

He had never had a girlfriend, had never gone on a date. Had worshipped girls from a distance but never approached them.

He said his prayers, the old prayers in French, praying, like Nina Citrone, for the children, and adding the soul of Mr. Zarbor. Slipping between the sheet and the blanket, he wondered about Nina Citrone's nightmares. She saw the crashing of the balcony. His nightmares were different. Vague: the children screaming, someone yelling "fire," a shadow chasing him. But the nightmare was not the worst part. The worst part came before he fell asleep or when he woke up in the middle of the night, when he heard again the noises in the balcony, what he had thought were rats scurrying through the rubbish and the junk. Maybe, if he had overcome his fear of rats and had gone up to the balcony, he might have found the weakness that caused it to collapse. He turned from the thought but, in the darkness of the room, the sound came back to him, that strange pulling-away sound.

He placed his hands over his ears to shut it out. Impossible, of course, because the sound was inside his mind, and along with it was the knowledge that maybe he was guilty after all, that his refusal to investigate the balcony had led to the deaths of the children. Nightmares ended when you woke up. Guilt never ended, worst in the dark of night but with you all the time, day or night.

Alone in the house the next morning, he answered Nina Citrone's letter. Poised with pen in hand and his mother's best stationery on the table, he did not know what to write. Actually, he knew why he was writing—to thank her for her letter—but how should he say it? Annoyed with himself, he wrote:

Dear Nina,

He did not really know her. Maybe he should call her Miss Citrone. He checked her letter. She had addressed him as John Paul.

Thank you very much for your letter.

That was safe. And proper.

It was kind of you to write.

He frowned, bothered by something. "Kind" seemed too stiff a word. He pondered this a moment, crossed out "kind" and replaced it with "nice," then crossed out "nice" and restored "kind." He would have to copy the letter over. He sighed, troubled. Then found a solution:

> It was nice and kind of you to write to me.
> It was also good of you to pray for the souls of the children. I pray for them, too.

So far, so good. Next:

> I am glad you were not hurt and escaped from the theater. I am sorry for your nightmares. I have them, too.

Maybe he should not have mentioned nightmares. But he wanted to show her she was not alone in this. He would not mention his guilt, however. He had not mentioned his guilt to anyone.

> My injuries are all healed now. I will be returning to school in five days, next Monday.

He paused and put down the pen, unsure about what he would write next. Knew what he wanted to write but did not wish to appear too . . . he groped for the word and found it: "forward." Then wrote the sentence anyway:

> I hope we see each other at school.

87

He studied the sentence for a while, then let it stand. It wasn't too forward. It was a polite sentence.

      Thank you again for your letter.

This sounded too formal, but he could not think of a better ending. He looked at her letter, to see what word she had used above her name. "Sincerely."

He then read her entire letter again, oddly moved, finding it difficult to swallow. He had received no get-well cards at the hospital from any of his classmates and understood why. He had only been a student at Wickburg Regional for a few weeks, and did not make friends easily. He was only a name to them. But Nina Citrone had recognized him as a person, had seen kindness in him that he had not known existed.

He ended the letter with:

                Very sincerely,
                John Paul Colbert

To the Editor:

      The city of Wickburg should be ashamed of itself for not pursuing further the investigation of the disaster at the Globe Theater on October 31. The probe seemed to die along with the death of the theater owner. But there was another person involved in this needless tragedy, the only person other than the theater owner who was in the theater in the months prior to the collapse of the balcony.

      That person is the young usher. Quotes from

initial stories showed that he was familiar with the balcony. He often went there to store material. He also was in the balcony minutes before the tragedy to check out "a sound." He lit the match that started the fire that might have initiated the plunging of the balcony on the innocent children below. "We have no evidence that the fire was connected with the balcony's collapse," the public safety commissioner reported. What does that mean? Exactly what it says. There is no evidence. This is obvious, because whatever evidence existed has been consumed in the flames and wreckage. If there is no evidence that the boy caused the collapse, there is also no evidence that he did not cause it or did not know about the condition of the balcony. "Case closed," the commissioner said after the death of Mr. Zarbor. This case will never be closed until justice is served.

D. C.

Wickburg

The newspaper trembled in his hands. He was alone in the house. He had heard the thump of the paper against the back door, thrown by the kid who delivered it every day. He brought it into the house, averting his eyes from the front page and the headlines, then told himself that he could not go through life avoiding newspapers. Glancing tentatively at the front page, he was relieved to find no story about the Globe. Same with page 2. He skipped to the sports page but was not interested in the Celtics or the Bruins. He and his father liked baseball, often watched the Red Sox games on television together. He flipped to the comics. Ran his eyes over the strips without enthusiasm. He was without enthusiasm for anything these days.

He seldom consulted the editorial page, although he sometimes glanced at the political cartoon or forced himself to read the editorial. "You must learn about your new country, and the newspaper is the best place," his father said. Dutifully, he scanned the editorial, something dull about wastewater treatment. His eye fell upon the Letters to the Editor space at the bottom of the page and the brief caption over the single letter printed there: "Case Open?"

After reading the letter, he dropped the newspaper to the carpet, knowing at last that the tragedy would go on forever, that he would have to live with it for the rest of his life.

That knowledge was lodged within him like a block of ice that would never melt.

On his first day back at school, John Paul was glad for the bigness of Wickburg Regional. The corridors were filled with hurrying students as the bells sounded at regular intervals. No one paid attention to him. Remembering the photograph in the newspaper, he tried to shrivel into himself, wishing himself invisible. He was relieved to find that students regarded him indifferently, as usual. He avoided looking into other people's eyes, even the teachers'.

The only awkward moment came when he reported to his homeroom. He became aware of eyes staring at him as he took his seat in the next-to-last row, near the window. He wondered if a father or mother of one of these students had written that letter to the editor.

Mr. Stein rapped on the desk with a ruler and

said: "We are happy to have you back, John Paul." Then glancing across the rows of students: "Isn't that right, class?" A demand in his voice.

"Right," someone called out, followed by other friendly greetings.

John Paul blushed furiously with both pleasure and embarrassment, as the bell rang for classes to begin.

As usual, he was not called upon to recite. A few classmates nodded at him, neither friendly nor unfriendly, just as they had before the tragedy. As he walked out of U.S. history, a kid he did not know grabbed his hand and pumped it. "Glad you're okay," he said.

Stunned, his palm instantly wet, John Paul managed to say, "Thank you."

He was stunned again during lunchtime when, eating alone, he saw the blond girl who had helped that day at the theater coming toward his table. He had looked up from the unappetizing hamburger plate—all food was still unappetizing to him—to see her heading his way, her eyes seeking his, her long blond hair bouncing lightly on her shoulders.

He rose to greet her.

She smiled at him, with her lips and her deep brown eyes, the eyes such a contrast to the fairness of her skin and her blond hair.

"Thanks for answering my letter," she said.

He felt his mouth drop open in astonishment. And could not close it, as if his jaw had frozen in place.

He had answered Nina Citrone's letter, not this girl whose name he didn't even know.

"Don't you remember me?" she said. "You must get a lot of mail. I'm Nina Citrone, from the theater . . ."

"Nina Citrone?" he said. Stumbling on her name, feeling stupid.

"Yes."

"But . . ."

"But what? . . ."

"You said I was kind and helpful that day . . ."

"Oh, but you were. I was terrified. My parents never let me work, never let me do anything, and all those kids, I was really nervous . . ."

"You did not look nervous . . ." Forgetting his contractions.

"I know. I put on this big act. Like before the oral book reports. Did I yawn? I have these terrible things I do, like yawn, when I'm nervous. Like talking to you now. Know what? My knees are shaking. And I'll probably yawn any minute . . ."

She began to yawn, maybe on purpose, and he joined her with a fake yawn and they laughed together, as if they were old friends or maybe more than friends. Clatters of dishes and metal trays faded in the distance as they walked out of the cafeteria together, talking, although later he could not remember what they said, except that she looked at him with a kind of tenderness in her eyes. He could not believe his good fortune, walking in the corridor with a beautiful girl beside him.

"I'm glad you're back," she said when they reached her homeroom. "Maybe we can sit together at lunch sometime."

He swallowed, took a big risk: "Tomorrow?"

"Okay," she said, and actually began to blush, her pale skin turning pink, a beautiful pink. With a sweet smile, she was gone.

Heart singing, light in his heart instead of darkness for the first time in ages, he made his way to his homeroom. Walked to his desk without worrying about whether anyone looked at him or not. Sat down and lifted the desktop to pick up his social studies textbook. Saw the sheet of paper on top of the book, the words written in blunt letters:

Welcome Back,
Killer.

Part Three

*D*enny Colbert stood in the kitchen of the apartment in Barstow waiting for the telephone to ring again. He had answered the day before for only the second time in his life, and the echo of that strange intimate voice still lingered in his mind. He was also exhilarated by the mere fact of finally having answered the phone, amazed that he had waited so long.

He went to the window and looked out, parting the white lace curtains. The neighborhood to which they had moved four months ago was a mixture of apartment buildings, some old, some new, with small neat lawns out front and space for small vegetable or flower gardens in the backyards.

Nothing of interest in the street. A woman leading a procession of four small children, linked by a length of clothesline. There was only one tree on the entire street, a scraggly, pathetic maple whose leaves, even in September, had begun to shrivel and turn brown at the edges. He remembered the girl at the bus stop and what she had said about him and the trees. He wondered whether the girl would show up again. He should have been nicer to her. Should have been more civil.

A thump from the porch brought him to the kitchen door. The *Barstow Patriot* lay in a plastic wrap on the porch floor.

He held the newspaper in his hand but did not unfold it, thinking of another newspaper headline from long ago, a headline he had thought was buried forever in the past but jarred loose now and vivid in his memory:

GLOBE HORROR LINGERS AFTER 20 YEARS

He had been eleven years old when he'd found out that his father had been involved in a tragedy in which twenty-two children died. He had read about it in a kitchen much like this one, startled to see his father's picture in the newspaper, his eyes zooming over the sentences as the cruel words leaped from the page—*bomb threats to his home . . . harassing telephone calls . . . hate mail . . .*

At last, he had finally learned the secret behind those middle-of-the-night calls, the mysterious letters, why they moved so often, why his father went from job to job. And why he seldom smiled and made such strict rules: *Don't answer the telephone, Denny. Don't let anyone in the house. Be careful whom you choose for friends.*

Denny shook his head as he thought of how he had lived with those rules, not daring to break them.

Until yesterday.

But I'm sixteen now—I want to be like other kids. Answer the telephone, get my license.

He looked at the telephone, silent, inanimate, wondering if it would ring again. Not sure whether he wanted it to ring. Jesus, what did he want, anyway?

I want to get out of here.

That's what he did. Put on the leather flight jacket that always cheered him up. Zipped it. Then out the door and down the stairs and into the street. Stood there, uncertain. He glanced at his watch. His mother wouldn't be home for another hour and a half, his father even later.

He caught a bus downtown and walked from the bus stop to the library. The whiff of books and bindings greeted him as he entered through the sliding doors, and he immediately thought of Chloe. They used to meet at the Bartlett Public Library, pretending to study and sometimes actually studying, other times writing notes to each other and sliding them across the glistening oak table. He didn't want to think of Chloe now, and he shut her out of his mind as he went to the desk and asked if his permanent library card had arrived. Not yet, the young librarian said. She was blond, and revealed dimples when she smiled. Her smile set off a glow within him until he noticed that she smiled automatically at everybody the same way.

No new 87th Precinct books in the mystery section. Or least none he had not read. The library buzzed with after-school activity, kids doing research or just hanging out.

Dust motes danced in the splashes of sunlight slanting through the windows. The memory of Chloe and that terrible school pageant clutched painfully at his heart. It had been a pageant dramatizing historical events in Worcester County: the Underground Railroad before the Civil War; Indian attacks on the town of Lancaster; the loss of Wickburg millionaire and philanthropist Daniel S. Hobart on the *Titanic;* and the reenactment of twenty-two children trapped in the Globe Theater fire and balcony collapse, in Wickburg, narrated by Chloe Epstein. Her words created an uproar when Denny's English teacher, Mr. Harper, leaped to his feet to denounce the presentation. "Don't you know what you've done to a student who's sitting right here in the auditorium?" Pointing to Denny and, despite his best intentions, bringing the spotlight of notoriety upon him.

Everybody had apologized later, Chloe in tears, almost hysterical—"I never connected your father with the tragedy" . . . "I thought the name was a coincidence" . . . "I'm so sorry, so sorry"—her words running into each other, stumbling over each other, grief ugly and raw on her face. He believed her, of course, but ruin had set in, his days at Bartlett Middle School spoiled forever as the story reached the newspapers and television, and Denny was weak with relief when his father said they were moving away. In the Bartlett Public Library, whispering furiously in a Saturday afternoon silence, he vowed to keep in touch with Chloe, said he would send her his address when his family got settled. But he never did.

Fleeing the library now and the memories, he caught a bus to his neighborhood but lingered in the street. The 24-Hour Store beckoned and he went inside, bought a Snickers, chewed it while perusing the magazines, aware of the store manager stationed at the cash register, glancing his way occasionally.

As he made his way to the doorway, he heard the manager say: "You live around here, don't you?"

Denny stopped in his tracks. He saw that the manager wasn't the manager, after all. His name was Dave and he was, as the badge on his lapel made known, the "Ass't. Mgr."

Puzzled as well as surprised, Denny said, "Yes, that gray three-decker down the street . . ."

"You don't want a job, do you?"

Really surprised this time.

Dave went on: "Big turnover here—I've only been here a month myself. The boss is always looking for more help, especially somebody in the neighborhood."

"I never worked in a store before," Denny said, angry at himself for what he was saying. Not the right time to be negative. "I never worked anywhere. I just turned sixteen . . ." Shut up, he told himself.

"You don't need experience on this job," Dave said. "The computer does it all for you. You punch in the amount, the computer tells you how much change to give. You don't even have to know how to add or subtract. You could flunk kindergarten and still do this job. Pretty good pay, too. Fifty cents an hour over the minimum. Name your own hours . . ."

He was about to say: I'll have to ask my father. Instead, he said: "I'll think about it . . ."

"Okay," Dave said. He seemed like a nice guy. "The boss is all right, leaves you pretty much alone. I've worked in a lot of stores, and I like it here. I think you will, too."

When another customer entered, Denny stepped away and had a chance to look more closely at the assistant manager. Something strange about his looks. Denny could not put his finger on it. Then did: that black hair. He was wearing a wig. Denny knew it was a wig because it was too perfect, too black, too shiny, like shoe polish. Did not match his eyebrows. Surprise: he had no eyebrows.

Dave had evidently caught his scrutiny. When the customer had left, he said: "What do you think of my roof?"

"Roof?"

Gesturing to his head, Dave said: "I underwent chemo and all my hair fell out. It's supposed to grow back better than ever, but not mine. Came back in clumps and patches. So I got this roof. Don't worry—it's not catching."

"What's not catching?" Denny asked, confused, uncomfortable at this sudden turn of the conversation.

"The Big One. What I've got. It's not contagious."

How could he be so cheerful?

"Hey, I'm in remission," Dave said, smiling, a weird smile. Those teeth, a perfect row of gleaming teeth. Dentures, of course. But the smile seemed genuine.

Denny thought how tough it must be to have the Big One, to undergo chemo—such a terrible word—and wear false hair, false teeth.

"You have to count your blessings," Dave said.

What blessings does Dave have? Denny wondered.

A flurry of customers now, and Denny made his getaway, breathless, the boredom of the afternoon and the uneasiness about the phone call fading as he pondered his strategy for getting his father's permission to work at the store.

* * *

"I've got a job," Denny announced at the dinner table, the words popping out of his mouth as spontaneously as a sneeze.

"What did you say?" his father asked, dropping his fork, which rattled on the plate.

His father seldom displayed any emotion and never showed surprise or disappointment. But Denny had scored with his announcement. His father's eyebrows drew together, forming a big black mustache over his eyes.

"A job," Denny said. "At the 24-Hour Store down the street. Part-time, after school . . ."

His father blew air out of his mouth and looked toward Denny's mother as if for support. Another surprise, since his father usually made all the decisions.

"We have not talked about this," his father said, his voice formal, his eyebrows back in their regular position. "This is an important step, Denny. You have to think of school, your grades, homework. You should have asked permission."

That word *permission* rankled him.

"You keep telling me that I should accept responsibilities, that I'm a young man now," Denny said, allowing himself for the first time in his life a display of anger toward his father. "But when I try to take responsibilities, like getting a job, you get mad."

"I'm not mad," his father said. "Surprised, yes. Disappointed, yes, because you didn't talk it over with us."

"How did this happen?" his mother asked, without rebuke or reproach in her voice. When Denny looked at her, he thought he saw some sort of approval in her eyes.

"I dropped into the store this afternoon and the assistant manager offered me a job. He said they're looking for someone from the neighborhood."

His father had not picked up his fork. The food lay neglected on his plate. His eyes were far away.

Denny knew he had deceived him. He had never lied to his father before, but at this particular moment he felt reckless, charged with energy. Without a shred of guilt. Maybe the guilt would come later. But right now: the hell with later.

"Look, Dad, I can earn my own way now. I won't have to ask for an allowance." Always humiliating, accepting money week after week, like a bribe for being a good son. "I can save for college." This last was stretching it a bit, but what the hell.

"Good, Denny," his mother said, looking at him with a hint of a smile, as if she was amused at that college remark but was going along with it. "I'm sure you'll be a great success no matter what you do."

Thanks, Mom.

"I suppose you *are* growing up," his father admitted, nodding his head in resignation.

Denny knew he had won, had scored a triumph over his father for the first time in his life. He drew a deep breath, concentrated on the plate before him, aware of his parents looking at him as if they had never looked at him before. He felt, strangely, a huge tenderness and love for them at this moment. Which did not prevent him from thinking:

Next move—my driver's license.

*T*he girl stood at the far end of the bus stop, staring across the street as if something very interesting was going on there. Denny followed her gaze and saw nothing unusual: apartment buildings, people going to work, a homeless man pushing a grocery cart carrying his belongings. Everything in quick tempo.

The girl's hair was pulled back into a ponytail, accenting her high and delicate cheekbones. She was even more beautiful than before.

Denny wondered if he should speak to her. Whether he should apologize. He wanted to celebrate the possible new job, wanted to share his good fortune with someone.

"Hey, Denny, your girlfriend's here," Dracula yelled.

Denny ignored the kid, his cheeks growing warm. The girl did not turn her head and made no comment, although she must have heard the little monster.

"Hey, Denny. I don't think she likes you," Dracula called out.

The awkward moment passed as the usual scuffle began, two monsters pushing and shoving each other. Dracula began to kick a kid Denny had never seen before—small, skinny, desperate on the pavement, clutching his stomach.

"Okay, break it up," Denny yelled, pulling the kids apart.

Before he could take any more action, the bus arrived in a belch of exhaust.

Denny helped the new kid to his feet. The boy, about ten years old, was trying to keep from crying, although tears already stained his cheeks. He pulled away when Denny started to brush the dirt from his jacket. "Leave me alone," he said. Typical, Denny thought. Learning young.

Denny was the last person to get on the bus. After flashing his ID at the driver, he shot a quick glance down the aisle and saw the girl settling into one of the rear seats.

Do I have the nerve? he wondered.

Because he felt reckless, he headed for the back of the bus and dropped into the seat beside the girl. Her bookbag was on the floor between her legs. This cheered him up. If she had really wanted to sit by herself, she would have placed the bookbag on the seat next to her.

Now what?

She surprised him by speaking first.

"I saw you break up that fight. Isn't that against your principles?"

"You set a good example the other day," he said. He hoped that was a good response.

She did not say anything.

"I'm not really one of the bad guys."

Still no answer.

"I'm trying to be civil." Emphasizing *civil.*

A small smile touched the edges of her mouth.

She still did not look at him, though.

"I'm thinking of starting a petition," he said. "Maybe you'll sign it."

"What kind of petition?"

"A petition to get the power companies to put the wires underground. So that they wouldn't hack the trees anymore." Was he overdoing this tree thing? But it was the only good thing he had going with her. "Also it would help during storms. With the lines underground, there'd be no falling trees or branches. Nobody's lights would go off." Then, trying for a joke: "You wouldn't have to watch television by candlelight." A line he'd heard somewhere—he hoped it sounded clever.

She looked at him. "I guess today you're Dr. Jekyll."

"Does that mean I was Mr. Hyde the other day?"

Her face turned serious, gray eyes probing his, turning blue suddenly.

"Which one is the real . . ." She let the sentence dangle.

"Denny Colbert," he said. "My name is really Dennis. My father came from Canada. He wanted my name to sound American and for some reason he thought Dennis was the epitome of American names." He liked using that word, *epitome*. He also felt ridiculous, knowing he was talking too much.

"My name is Dawn," she said. Then spelled it out: "*D-A-W-N*."

Dawn: beautiful. Like her. Sunrise, full of hope, Dawn. "That is a beautiful name," he said.

"My name is actually Donna, which I hate. Everybody was named either Donna or Debbie the year I was born. So I changed it. I mean, I looked in a mirror one day when I was eleven years old and thought: I am not a Donna . . . I'm a Dawn . . ."

He relaxed and soon felt comfortable with her, and they fell into an easy conversation. He learned, almost immediately, that they had something in common: she, too, was new to Barstow, her father having been transferred from Rhode Island when his engineering plant opened new territory in central Massachusetts. She said she found it difficult to make friends. Girls, she thought, were more snobbish than boys. More critical of each other. Did not accept newcomers easily.

"Or am I being too harsh on the members of my own sex?"

"I don't know," he said. "My family moves a lot. I've been to three schools already. So I don't try to make friends anymore. Because here today, gone tomorrow." Which sounded fake and dramatic but was the truth. But not all of the truth.

She asked the fatal question that he should have seen coming from a mile away.

"Why have you moved so much? Because of your father's job?"

He nodded. "My father gets restless." Big lie. "He likes to travel." Bigger lie. "But he wants to settle down here in Barstow." This one was the truth. "He has a new job that he likes, with opportunities for the future." Half-lie, half-truth.

"What does he do?"

Why did I sit down with her?

But he knew why: she was beautiful, those gray-blue eyes like no eyes he had ever seen before.

"He's in plastics." Safe answer. Half the workers in Barstow were in plastics, the factories inflicting millions of plastic articles, from toys to office equipment, on the world. "He's an expert on molding machines that turn out the plastics. They break down, he repairs them."

They lapsed into silence watching the world of Barstow lumber by. A beautiful day, really—sun radiant, splashing on the windows. The world inside the bus had diminished. Their seat was an island, an oasis, disconnected from everything else.

He learned that she lived in the same section of town as him. He told her about his job possibility. She said that she was sometimes sent to the 24-Hour Store when her mother forgot something or other at the supermarket. She was a sophomore at Barstow High, an okay school but nothing special. She asked him about Normal Prep. "I hear it's *ab*normal," she said, a joke. "My description exactly," he replied. They talked like old friends. He was madly in love, knees weak, stomach churning. Suddenly the bus arrived at Barstow High. She gathered her bookbag and got up.

Gulping, he seized the moment: "See you tomorrow?"

"Oh," she said, startled. "Guess not. My dad usually drives me to school. He passes by the same time the bus gets here. I only take this bus when he goes out of town."

"Oh." Felt stupid, mouth open.

"See ya," she said. Cruel, cruel words.

Slinging her bookbag over her shoulder, she made for the door. He wanted to call her back, say something, detain her. But didn't. And she was gone.

Not until later did he realize he didn't know her last name or where she lived.

The day continued to go downhill after that.

Sitting in the bleachers during lunch hour, he heard sudden sounds from below: scuffling, a bellow of pain and protest, a thud. He walked toward the end of the bleachers, peered around the corner and saw, thirty feet away, two Normal students being not so normal: beating up a third student. Not exactly beating him up but pushing and shoving him all over the place. Denny recognized the victim as a kid in U.S. history: Lawrence Hanson.

The scene was ludicrous: three guys neatly dressed in Norman Prep uniforms, clean-cut and regular-looking, acting like street-corner goons. Denny watched, fascinated, heart accelerating. *I'd better get out of here.* But didn't leave. Like being attracted to the scene of an accident.

Lawrence Hanson did not retaliate as the taller of his two assailants began to slap his face. First one cheek, then the other. Lawrence's hands were straight down his sides. Red stains appeared on his cheeks. The second assailant stepped in and began pushing against Lawrence's chest. Lawrence stumbled backward, still accepting the blows. *Why doesn't he fight back?*

At that moment, Lawrence looked in Denny's direction, and their eyes locked. Denny wasn't sure what he saw in those eyes, particularly at this distance. But he could see something. Fear, sure. Anger? Denny turned away. *This is not my business; it's got nothing to do with me.* He got out of there, tripping and stumbling as he made his way back to the school, trying to decipher Lawrence Hanson's expression.

Later, between social studies and math II, classes he didn't share with Lawrence Hanson, he met him face-to-face in the corridor. He looked normal enough except for a small swollen patch near his left eye. Denny opened his mouth to say something—but what? They stood facing each other for an excruciating moment. Denny was surprised by the anger in Hanson's eyes, as if Denny were the enemy, not the two guys who had assaulted him. Denny had left the scene, yes, but Hanson had refused to fight back. *All I did was mind my own business.*

After classes, crossing the quad, Denny spotted Jimmy Burke coming his way. He didn't want an encounter with him at this moment. Had no answer for him. Not yet, if ever. Denny changed direction, headed for the administration building as if he had an important errand to run. Thought he heard Jimmy Burke calling his name but kept on going.

Later, on the bus, he slumped in his seat, dejected and angry, not sure why he was angry or who he was angry with.

*   *   *

The day did not brighten but continued its dark descent when he stopped in at the 24-Hour Store and found an older man, a fringe of gray hair surrounding his bald head, behind the counter. The owner, probably.

Denny waited until the customers had departed before stepping up. He cleared his throat, hoping his voice wouldn't betray his nervousness.

"My name is Denny Colbert," he said. "The assistant manager said that I might be able to work here."

"Oh, yes," the man said, frowning. "My name is Arthur Taylor—this is my store. Dave told me about you."

He scratched his bald head. "Dave's an enthusiastic kind of guy. But he gets carried away sometimes. Sure, we get quite a turnover here, but there's nothing open at the moment. How old are you?" All in one quick breath.

"Sixteen." Disappointment causing him to almost stammer.

"Let me explain how this works, Denny. I try to hire older, more experienced people. There's a lot of responsibility in a job like this. Sometimes you have to work alone. You never know who's coming through that door." Pausing, apparently noticing Denny's disappointment, he said: "I'm sorry, son." Kindly, sympathetic. Then, sighing: "Okay, why don't you fill out an employment form. Maybe I can find a spot for you sometime."

Denny took the form and slipped it into one of his books. He suspected that the store owner was letting him down easy. A kind man, but no job to give out.

"Good ol' Dave," Mr. Taylor said, shaking his head. "I guess he took a liking to you. Drop around now and then, son, although I can't make any promises."

Denny was glad when a customer came in and he was able to make his getaway.

At home, the telephone rang as he poured himself a glass of orange juice. He drank the juice slowly, listening to the rings. Counted them as usual. *If it goes beyond ten, I'll answer it,* he thought. He walked toward the telephone, counting: eight, nine. As he reached to pick it up, the ringing stopped. He picked it up anyway and heard the dial tone, feeling a pang of loss although he couldn't imagine over what.

The next afternoon, as he sat at his desk pondering a math problem that had no importance in his life except for a mark on his report card, he heard someone knocking at the kitchen door. Sharp, insistent raps. Then silence. He waited, pen poised over the page. The knocking resumed. Dropping the pen, he made his way to the kitchen.

Knock knock, who's there?

He and his parents had had no visitors since moving to Barstow. Nobody from UPS had delivered a package. Mail was left in the standard metal box on the first-floor porch.

More knocks. One, two, three, four.

I'll huff and I'll puff and I'll blow your house down.

A muffled voice came from the other side of the door. Denny strained to listen. Heard the voice say: "It's important. Please open up."

A man's voice. Not a woman's. Definitely not a woman. Not the telephone caller. He stood uncertainly at the kitchen table. He did not want to open the door. *Who knows who might be standing there, only a few feet away?*

Cut the dramatics, he told himself. This is the middle of the afternoon and someone is merely knocking at the door. Could be a salesman. Or an emergency: a neighbor in desperate need of help. What had the knocker said? *"It's important. Please open up."*

Denny opened the door. Just a crack. Peered suspiciously through the narrow opening. Saw a middle-aged man, horn-rimmed glasses, gray hair, jacket pocket jammed with pens and pencils. Knew instantly who this was: a reporter. Remembered his father's command: *If approached, tell them nothing. Never say yes. Always say no. Or don't know.*

"Is Mr. Colbert at home?" the reporter asked.

Denny shook his head, began to close the door.

"Wait . . . Do you know when he's expected?"

The reporter's air of urgency stopped Denny's hand. More than that: this reporter seemed like a nice guy. Looked tired. His eyes bloodshot, as if he had not slept the night before. Denny knew that look, had seen it on his father's face.

"I don't know," Denny said. A stupid answer. Of course he knew when his father would come home. *After work.* Stupid question, too. The reporter should know that his father worked at Madison Plastics and would not be found at home in the middle of the afternoon.

"Actually, I wanted to talk to *you*," the reporter said. "You're Dennis Colbert, aren't you? I'm from the *Wickburg Telegram*."

"I'm sorry," Denny said. "I'm busy."

And began to close the door again.

"Wait a minute," the reporter said. "I want to help. I want to help you, and your father."

"We don't need your help," Denny said, his reply fueled by the memory of that blazing headline and story in the *Telegram* years ago. Maybe this reporter had written that story, that headline.

"I think you do," the reporter said. But speaking kindly, not threatening. And also speaking wearily, sighing. "Would you please listen to me for a minute?"

Denny's impulse to close the door was overwhelmed by curiosity. Maybe the reporter could tell him things his father had never revealed to him. Maybe he could help, after all.

"In a week or two, there're going to be big stories about the Globe tragedy," the reporter said. "Your father's an important part of that story. My paper's the biggest in Worcester County, Dennis. And my editor wants to pull out all the stops. He assigned me to head the team working on the story. Interviewing the survivors. Tracking down relatives of the victims. But my editor also wants drama. By drama, he means sleaze. Know what sleaze is, Dennis?"

Denny did not answer, riveted by the reporter's words, immersed in his father's tragedy.

"Sleaze is a lousy approach to news. Started by TV.

Gossip, innuendo . . . the worse the better. *Inside Story. Tough Copy.* No holds barred, kid. The sleazier the better. So, newspapers have to keep up with the sleaze factor. Your father's the only living survivor of the scandal—theater owner's dead, city inspector's dead, even the investigator's dead. That leaves your father. The problem, kid, is your father isn't talking. When someone tracks him down, he always says: 'No comment.' That makes him fair game. And, frankly, I think it's going to be brutal this time. For him, for your mother, for yourself. It's the twenty-fifth anniversary."

The reporter spoke quietly, sympathetically, in contrast to the cruel words that came out of his mouth.

"What can I do to help?" Denny asked. Yet felt it was a useless question.

"Your father has never given an interview in all these years, and I respect him for that. But that means he never gave his side of the story. The human side. People have never found out what kind of man he is. What kind of family he has. Maybe a story from you can humanize him. Maybe if you tell us about him it will help. What do you say, Dennis?"

"I don't know what to say," Denny said. "My father always told me not to talk about it to anybody. Not even to answer the phone."

A light leaped in the reporter's eyes. "That's the kind of thing I need, Dennis. The fact that he's trying to protect you, *protect his family*. This can give the public an entirely different picture of your father. Right now, a lot of people wonder about him. He's mysterious, and it's easy to make him a scapegoat. We can change that around. Our story can be first, can set the pace for other newspapers, television, radio . . ."

"I don't know," Denny said. He was afraid he was betraying his father by talking to this reporter.

"What's your name?" he asked, stalling, having to say something.

"Les Albert." The reporter searched his pockets, came up with a limp, soiled card. "Here's my card. The *Telegram*'s phone number, too. Think it over, Dennis. Call me. Collect. If I don't hear from you, I'll drop by again. But time is a factor."

"I don't know," Denny said, aware that he was repeating himself, must appear slow and stupid. Yet the reporter, with his sad, red-streaked eyes, seemed sympathetic.

"Trust me," Les Albert said. "I mean it."

That was the problem, Denny thought, as he closed the door: could he really trust him?

He listened to the reporter's footsteps receding, the porch door opening and closing. In the living room, he looked out the window, waited patiently. After a few minutes, Les Albert emerged from the shadows of the driveway and walked to a car parked at the curb. An old model, nondescript, faded green. He took a camera from the car and swung it toward the house. Denny drew back, let the curtain fall into place. Although he was out of sight, he felt exposed and defenseless.

He took out the reporter's card and began tearing it in two, but stopped. He found some Scotch tape in his desk and repaired the card, then slipped it into his wallet.

*   *   *

117

Next day, more knocking as he walked by the 24-Hour Store and turned to see assistant manager Dave rapping on the window, beckoning him inside. Denny hesitated, then entered.

"I'm sorry about the job," Dave said. "I didn't realize Mr. Taylor wasn't hiring teenagers." He patted his roof as if to make sure it was still there.

"That's okay," Denny said, although it wasn't. He felt as if somehow Dave had betrayed him.

"Sounds like age discrimination, doesn't it?" Dave said, obviously trying to be friendly.

Denny didn't feel friendly. "Maybe I ought to sue," he said, remembering when "This Litigious Society" had been the topic in social studies for an entire week. "For a million dollars."

"I'd be a great witness for your side," Dave said brightly.

They both laughed at the prospect. Looking at Dave's pathetic wig, like a black pancake on his head, the false teeth, the eyes begging for forgiveness, Denny could not remain angry.

"I think you should make it two million," Dave said.

"Or three," Denny added.

They both started laughing, caught up in the absurdity of it all, and Denny felt drawn to the strange man. He decided to hang out at the store for a while. He had no one else to talk to during the long afternoons after school anyway.

*   *   *

Denny and his mother went to church every Sunday. His father never went to mass. "Why?" Denny asked as they walked to St. Martin's Church.

"Your father is religious in his own way," she said. "He doesn't go to mass, but he prays." She did not say anything for a while and then said: "I think, Denny, he has his own church: the cemetery in Wickburg where most of the children are buried, the children who died at the Globe. He used to disappear every Saturday for a few hours, even when we lived in Bartlett. Finally, he told me where he went. To the cemetery. Where he prayed for the souls of the children. That's his church, Denny, that cemetery."

A sudden memory came clear: "He took me there once when I was a little kid," Denny said. "I remember we knelt down. I remember that there were tears in his eyes. But he didn't explain why we were there. I must have been only five or six years old . . ."

"He still goes there once in a while, Denny." She touched his shoulder, as if trying to create a bridge between her and him and, by extension, his father. "He's such a good man, your father. He . . ." Her voice trailed off.

"What?" Denny asked. "He . . . what?" Sensing that his mother wanted to say more.

"I was thinking of that terrible day at the Globe. The first time I saw him. He wasn't like other guys at school, in my neighborhood. He seemed to care. About those children. Even about us, the helpers. Trying to do his best. He was . . ." She paused, as if searching for the right word: "Nice. I know that doesn't sound glamorous, Denny.

But that's exactly what your father was, still is—a nice guy."

She stopped walking, turned toward him. "I never told him what I saw that day. I saw the balcony crash down. I saw him falling with it, saw him swallowed up in all that debris. I thought he'd been killed, that nice guy I'd just met. Later, when I found out he was alive and heard the accusations people were making, I wrote him a letter . . ."

"And the rest is history, right?" he said, keeping his voice light but oddly touched that his mother had shared this memory with him.

A sudden rising wind hastened them along the street. His mother looked up at the clear blue sky. "Oh, Denny, maybe this year will be different. Maybe it won't be like other years . . ."

Denny didn't say anything, did not want to spoil this beautiful moment on the way to church.

*T*he telephone rang almost every afternoon now but Denny ignored it, using all his old defenses: flushing the toilet in the bathroom, turning up the volume on the radio, or, finally, leaving the apartment.

On the street, he faced several choices, none of them exciting. Once or twice, he walked the streets of the neighborhood, beginning with the adjacent ones and then branching out, searching for Dawn, his lost friend from the bus. Which was ridiculous, in a way. The odds against spotting her were enormous unless he got lucky and walked by her house at the moment she came out the door or happened to be raking the lawn. Most of the lawns and sidewalks were covered with leaves, some of them beautiful in their hectic colors, but Denny didn't respond to their beauty. Falling leaves meant October, and October meant

Halloween, which also meant the coming anniversary. Soon, Halloween decorations would begin to appear, and he'd ignore them, too.

He usually dropped into the 24-Hour Store after school, although he had given up any hope of being hired. Sometimes Dave wasn't working. Or he was too busy for conversation, or appeared distracted and withdrawn, as if he had worries on his mind. Other times, he greeted Denny warmly and could be entertaining.

Once he told Denny he did a lot of traveling between jobs or on vacations and had a hobby: tracking down unusual statues all over the world. He ignored statues of generals and politicians, he said, but loved, for instance, the statue in Dublin, Ireland, of a woman who sold fish from a wagon. "Imagine that, Denny: a statue to Molly Malone, who wheeled her wheelbarrow through streets broad and narrow . . ." Singing the words in a high tenor voice, forgetting to touch his roof but his dentures gleaming in the fluorescent light. Denny glanced out the window now and then, hoping to see Dawn nearing the store, or looked with anticipation toward the door when it opened, hoping to see her come in.

At Normal Prep, he went through all the proper motions. Minded his own business, as usual. Avoided the bleachers after lunch, finding a quiet spot to study. Studying, particularly doing his homework, was the key— knowing the information so that he passed the tests, knew the answers when teachers called upon him in class, did not force attention on himself. Jimmy Burke pulled him aside once as he left school.

"Still marking time?" Jimmy asked. Denny thought

about Lawrence Hanson under the bleachers, not fighting back.

"Elections are coming up next week," Jimmy said.

Denny shrugged. "Let me think about it," he said.

"Great," Jimmy responded, his enthusiasm blazing in the air.

I only said I'd *think* about it, Denny told himself as he turned away, a bit flustered at the opening he'd given Jimmy Burke.

The *Barstow Patriot* always arrived before his parents came home and Denny would check it out, grateful every day at the absence of a story about the anniversary. Now, at the 24-Hour Store, he glanced through the *Wickburg Telegram,* looking for Les Albert's byline, his heart leaping at the sight of it. The reporter was writing a series of stories on arson in low-income housing projects in Worcester County.

Once in a while, he took out Les Albert's card and looked at it, wondering whether he should take up the reporter on his offer. He'd be able to tell his father's side of the tragedy, show that his father was a good man, hard-working, a little stiff and formal maybe, but kind and gentle in his own way. Denny wasn't sure that was the kind of thing the reporter wanted for a story, despite what he'd said. Aside from the occasional phone calls and letters, his father's life was, well, *b-o-r-i-n-g.* Denny always ended up not doing anything about the reporter's request. Told himself he was merely postponing the decision. Then placed the card back in his wallet.

* * *

"When do you start your new job?" his father asked, catching Denny off guard.

After learning from Mr. Taylor that the job was not available and with dim hopes that he would ever be hired, Denny had avoided the topic when he was with his parents, had been relieved when his father made no inquiry.

But now his question stopped Denny cold as he made his way through the living room after supper. He had planned to start the campaign for his driver's license tonight, having figured out a compromise: applying for a learner's permit, which would allow him to at least start driving lessons. But suddenly he was on the defensive.

"There's no job," he admitted, looking away from his father's direct gaze. "The guy who offered me the job had the wrong information. The store doesn't hire teenagers, only old people."

"You told us that you were hired," his father said.

Denny forced himself to look into his father's eyes. "I thought I was," he said, realizing how one lie leads to another, with maybe more to come.

"But now you're not." His father's voice was edged with sarcasm. Does he suspect me of lying? Denny wondered.

"This guy was only the assistant manager. He didn't know about the policy."

His father looked at him for what seemed a long time. Then: "Too bad . . ."

Denny was taken by surprise, because his father seemed to be genuinely sympathetic.

He decided to push his luck.

"Maybe there'll be openings at the mall . . ."

A frown crossed his father's face, and he turned to pick up his newspaper. "That, I think, would be a problem. The mall is too far to go."

Denny knew that he had said the wrong thing. He also knew that tonight was not the right time to bring up the learner's permit.

At the bus stop, the monsters behaved like monsters as usual, jostling each other, pushing, shoving, swearing. Every morning somebody was knocked to the pavement.

"Hey, Denny, is your girlfriend mad at you?" Dracula called out, causing a sudden silence and a halting of activity while everybody looked at him. "She don't show up anymore."

Denny ignored him.

Which only encouraged the monster to continue.

"Guess she found another guy, right, Denny? A goodlooking guy this time, right, Denny? Like a guy with a car, right, Denny?"

Denny envisioned himself walking over to the monster, knocking him down with a vicious blow to the jaw, leaping on him, strangling him slowly while the kid turned blue, struggling at first, then dying slowly, painfully.

Then he told himself to forget it: he was a monster all right, but still just a kid.

One afternoon, he stood outside Barstow High School in another attempt to find Dawn. He had discovered that Normal Prep's school day ended a half hour earlier than Barstow High's and that he could, with luck and perfect timing, reach Dawn's school a minute or two before hundreds of students burst out of the place as classes ended for the day.

He had stationed himself in front of the school near the nine orange buses whose engines throbbed while waiting for their passengers. Denny figured Dawn would be getting on one of the buses.

The bell rang, once, twice, three times, and doors all over the building flew open, followed by a wave of students, going in all directions as if sprayed from a hose. Denny's eyes darted here, there and everywhere as crowds of students headed for the buses. He saw a lot of girls— short, tall, dark, light, in jeans, skirts, one blond girl in a flowered dress that reached her ankles—but no Dawn.

Ten minutes later, the buses had lumbered away, engines roaring, gears grinding. Denny felt suddenly conspicuous standing on the sidewalk in his Norman Prep uniform, a stranger among the few stragglers who lingered in front of the school. His big chance had passed. Loneliness clutched him. Along with the knowledge that he faced a three-mile walk home. Alone.

*F*inally, he answered the afternoon call.

He had not planned to do it, was used to hearing it ring every day. Why did he pick up the phone at that particular moment?

He didn't know why, exactly.

He was lonesome in the empty apartment, was not in the mood for homework, not in the mood for anything.

At that moment the phone rang.

Without thinking of the consequences, he picked it up.

He pressed the receiver to his ear, did not speak, did not say hello. And, thrilled, heard that smoky voice:

"Is that you, Denny? I hope it's you. I can hear you breathing."

He drew in his breath and still did not say anything.

"Please don't hang up, Denny, like last time. I've been calling and calling, wanting to talk to you so badly . . ."

Still said nothing. Hypnotized by her voice, her words. *Wanting to talk to you.*

"Aren't you lonesome? Alone every afternoon? New in town and no friends to talk to . . ."

How does she know all that? he wondered.

"Who are you?" he asked. Maybe she'd tell him this time.

"Someone just like you. Who knows how it is to be alone."

"Are you the same person who calls my father during the night?"

The question came out of his mouth as spontaneously and unplanned as his act of picking up the phone had been.

Big pause. Her turn to be silent. The shoe on the other foot, as his father would say.

"I think a lot of people call your father, Denny."

"Why do *you* call him?" he asked, softening his voice but sensing that he was on the right track with this line of questioning.

"I don't know about the others. I only know that I can't sleep at night and that's why I call."

"That's a rotten thing to do. Do you know what it feels like to hear a phone ring like that in the middle of the night? My father hardly sleeps anymore."

"But I'm calling *you* now," she said. "Daytime, afternoon . . ."

He sighed, and his question came on the breath of that

sigh. "Why?" His anger spent, genuinely curious. Why should she be calling him?

"I want to get to know you, Denny. And maybe you can get to know me . . . and if you get to know me, you might understand a lot of things you don't understand now."

"What things?"

"Maybe I'll tell you the next time I call. Will you talk to me again, Denny? I have so much I want to tell you . . ."

"I don't know," he said, and hung up abruptly, just as he had spontaneously picked up the telephone a few moments earlier.

That boy's voice, Lulu says, *so sweet, such a sweet voice.*

But Lulu's voice is not so sweet, and I see what is flashing in her eyes, the mischief there. More than mischief: malice. Mischief is playful but the thing in Lulu's eyes is not playful at all.

Such a nice boy, Lulu says, her voice flat and deadly and not nice at all.

Are you going through with it, then, Lulu? I ask.

Was there ever any doubt, Baby?

She still calls me Baby, but not tenderly like in the old days. We laughed a lot in those days, and loved the same things and practically thought the same thoughts. She says she still loves me and that she has taken care of me in my dark days and so I must take care of her through her own darkness.

Are you still going to help me, Baby?

He's such a nice kid, Lulu. You said that yourself. I'd hate to see him in pain.

He won't have any pain, she says. *But the pain of his father, that will last forever. The pain of knowing that his son is paying for what he did.*

I know my words will be useless, having been said so many times, but I have to say them:

The father didn't do anything, Lulu. The authorities cleared him.

And her answer is the same:

The authorities! Speaking with contempt. *They covered up. Politicians always cover up. He was in the balcony and he started the fire and the balcony fell down on us. One and one, Baby, still adds up to two.*

Then, going to the window and looking out, she says, *I don't want to talk about it anymore.*

I know what she really does not want to talk about, that one thing like a shadow that has fallen between us, separating us from what we used to be and what we are now.

She will not talk about what happened to her while she was dead.

What she saw and did.

Whether she was in heaven or hell. Or limbo, the place Aunt Mary told us little babies went to who aren't baptized.

Lulu used to joke with her about that, but a serious kind of joking.

You mean, she'd say to Aunt Mary, *that babies can't get into heaven because a priest didn't splash them with water?*

That was my old Lulu, fresh and sassy.

I'm only saying what the church teaches, Aunt Mary would respond.

I like the thought of limbo, though, Lulu would say. *Neither heaven nor hell. Sounds like a great place to be.*

I wonder if limbo is where Lulu went. But she won't talk about it.

Other people talk about it, I tell her. *They see a beautiful light. They float and drift. They feel happy and contented and don't want to come back.*

She only stares at me with those terrible eyes filled with something I can't describe, her mouth a cruel slash and her cheeks taut. Her face like a mask that hides the real Lulu, my old Lulu who used to tickle me and make me laugh.

That Lulu is gone.

And this new Lulu makes me lie awake at night, and makes me hide what I'm writing so that she can't see it.

Part Four

With Halloween approaching, the color scheme everywhere in Barstow was orange for pumpkins, black for witches and white for ghosts. The warmth of September had surrendered to chilled October days and nights, sudden winds which brought leaves down extravagantly, and dull slate skies. No rain, however, and everything crisp, autumn-toasted leaves creating small whirlwinds before littering the streets and sidewalks.

Denny trekked homeward from the bus stop, kicking absently at the leaves. He shook his head in disapproval at the pumpkins on doorsteps. The latest craze: painting weird faces on pumpkins. He remembered his father patiently scooping the pulp out of a pumpkin, painstakingly carving out eyes, a nose and a gap-toothed mouth. A candle placed inside brought it spookily to life. He wondered whether he was too old to ask his father to carve him a pumpkin this year.

Passing by the 24-Hour Store, he saw that Mr. Taylor, not Dave, was standing at the cash register. Disappointed, he turned toward home. As he turned into the driveway, he checked his watch: 2:46. Time to spare. Lulu always called between 3:00 and 3:30, never earlier, never later.

At home, the pulse in his temple leaped erratically as he climbed the stairs thinking of Lulu. He opened the screen door and was instantly nauseated.

Later, he wasn't sure which came first, the terrible smell or the sight of what was piled on the doorstep. Probably both at once. Retching miserably at the banister, unable to vomit despite his nausea, he knew that his hopes for the twenty-fifth anniversary's passing without incident had probably ended. There had been only two nighttime phone calls in the past week. Only one letter, which his father flushed down the toilet without opening. No publicity at all. The reporter from the *Wickburg Telegram* had not returned and there had been no approaches from the television or radio stations. Best of all: his own telephone calls. From her. That voice, those words. He had hoped, vaguely, that in some way those calls had stopped all the mischief.

But what he found on the doorstep filled him with dread.

What next?

Before thinking about that, he had to clean up the mess before his mother and father got home.

He went down to the cellar, looking for something to pick it up with. Under the stairs, he found an empty shoe box. Tore down one side to form a kind of dustpan. Would use the cover as a brush to scoop it up. Went upstairs, dreading the sight and stench of what was waiting for him.

Taking a deep breath, he swept it into the box, missing some, of course, doing it again, trying to avert his eyes, trying not to breathe but breathing anyway. He knew he would have to scrub the stoop later with soap and water.

Standing there with the reeking shoe box, he thought: Now what do I do?

He did the obvious—flushed it down the toilet, rinsed the box, scrubbed the doorstep with an old rag, placed box, cover and rag in a plastic bag and dropped it into one of the rubbish barrels in the driveway.

Back in the apartment, he waited as usual for the telephone to ring. He skipped his after-school lunch, his stomach still queasy from the chore he had just performed but his heart fluttering, anticipating Lulu's voice on the telephone.

He sat in his father's chair, next to the end table on which the telephone stood. He took off his watch and propped it against the phone, the better to see it. 3:09. The phone could ring anytime now.

3:16.

The apartment still, like a museum after hours.

3:21.

She might not call today. She sometimes skipped a day or two.

Restless, he got up, stretched, yawned that old boredom yawn, went to the porch door, swung it open, looked down to see if any stain remained. He shuddered, recalling the smell, as fresh now as at the moment of discovery.

He remembered what Lulu had once said about people doing things to his father.

A devastating thought:

Had Lulu placed that pile of stench on the doorstep?

Was it her shit he had flushed down the toilet?

No, it couldn't be.

She could never do such a thing.

Not Lulu.

"Lulu."

He said her name aloud, loved the sound of it. She hadn't told him her name at first, seemed reluctant to identify herself, which added to the mystery of her calls. But she'd finally told him.

She'd been teasing him about his own name. She said she preferred Col-*bair* to Colbert. "Colbert is so hard and harsh, but Col-*bair* is soft and French and . . ."

He caught the beginning sound of an *s*, and wondered, excited, whether she was about to say "sexy."

Flustered, he said: "You know my name but I don't know yours . . ."

"Do you want to know my name?"

"Yes."

"That makes me happy, Denny. Makes me feel that I mean something to you, that I'm more than just a voice."

Thrilled and embarrassed, puzzled that he should be thrilled and embarrassed, he said, "I like talking to you."

"I do, too. In fact, I like *you*, Denny."

He figured she was avoiding his question, did not really want to tell him her name.

But she surprised him:

"Lulu. Call me Lulu."

Call me Lulu . . .

"Is that your name or just what people call you?"

"Lulu is my special name. Only people who are close to me call me Lulu. And you're close to me, Denny. So close . . ."

Aroused, looking down at himself—what's happening here, what's happening to me?—he could not speak.

"Denny, are you still there? I hear you breathing—are you all right? Did I say something wrong?"

"No," he said, the word strangling in his throat as he tried to bring himself under control.

She always spoke softly, breathlessly, as if there were no one in the world except the two of them. As if they were friends—no, more than friends: as if they shared deep secrets. That smoky voice.

She made a dull day dance, made the most ordinary things sound exciting. Like September.

She was sad about September because it was over.

"Like a lovely woman gone away," she said.

"A woman?"

"Yes, September's like a woman. Beautiful. Voluptuous. You know what voluptuous means, don't you, Denny?"

"Of course," he said, heart racing: *voluptuous,* conjuring up visions of beautiful women, knowing in his heart that Lulu must be beautiful, too. And voluptuous.

Lulu's voice was mesmerizing, a hypnotist's voice—*you are getting sleepy, sleepy . . .* —but he wasn't sleepy at all, exactly the opposite, wide awake, every pore open, soaking her words and her voice into every part of his body, and his body responding. He squeezed his thighs together.

"October's a woman, too, Denny. But a witch. A ghost or a goblin. That's why I don't like October, hate it, because it ends with Halloween." Her voice was suddenly bitter, sending chills through his bones. Then warm again and playful: "What month do you think I am, Denny?"

He thought of frigid January and warm July, hot August, himself suddenly hot and perspiring, as if August had arrived. He swallowed hard, squirming, the words not coming at all.

"I hope you think I'm September, Denny, and not February, not cold and freezing . . ."

"September," he said, stammering a bit, heart tumbling inside of him, like a September leaf in the wind. Finding the courage, at last, to say: "Yes, definitely September."

* * *

He wondered how old she was. Her voice provided no clue. If she'd been calling his father all these years, she couldn't be young. But a part of him denied that she could be old. He wanted her to be young.

Finally, mustering his courage, he asked: "How old are you, Lulu?" He loved saying her name.

"How old do you think I am?"

Like a teacher, answering a question with another question. But never a teacher in school like Lulu.

"I don't know." Not daring to guess.

"When you hear the sound of my voice, Denny, do you think I'm old? Or young?"

"Young." Hoping.

"Ah, Denny . . ."

She *had* to be young.

"Do I sound nice? Or not so nice?"

"Nice," he said. Said it again: "Nice."

"That's good. I want you to think I'm nice. So that you'll keep talking to me. I look forward to these calls. The days when I can't call you, I feel lonesome . . ."

"I do, too," he heard himself saying.

"Know what, Denny? I don't call your father at night anymore. Maybe other people call him, but I don't. Know why?"

"No."

"Because I'd rather talk to you. I like talking to you . . ."

"I like to talk to you, too," he said, wondering if she heard the tremor in his voice, if she knew what was happening to him.

And didn't care whether she was young or old.

*   *   *

Now he looked at the clock.

3:31.

Today's big moment hadn't arrived. She hadn't called. The apartment, suddenly desolate, the bright sun mocking him as it splashed on the carpet. Should be raining to match his mood.

He drilled his eyes at the phone, commanding it to ring.

But it didn't.

"*H*ey, Denny, I saw your sweetheart the other day."

Dracula stopped pummeling Son of Frankenstein to make the announcement.

Denny pretended indifference, acted as if he had not heard what Dracula said. He did not trust the little monster. Even at twelve years old, he had the manner of a gangster from old movies, and looked, in fact, like a juvenile James Cagney.

Even *sweetheart* was a James Cagney kind of word.

"Where did you see her?" he said, voice crackling, which did not help his act of indifference very much.

"I dunno," Dracula said, bored with hitting Son of Frankenstein and turning toward Denny. "Downtown."

"Where downtown?" Denny said, controlling his voice.

"I dunno. Kenton's Department Store."

Denny didn't say anything for a few seconds. He did not want to appear too eager, sensing that Dracula would shut up if he thought Denny was really interested. Finally, he said: "What was she doing there?"

Dracula looked at him with suddenly innocent eyes. "In the department store?" He knocked Son of Frankenstein to the pavement.

"Yes," Denny said patiently. A twelve-year-old James Cagney but the cold eyes of a forty-year-old hit man.

"She was working, I think. She was standing behind the counter. The perfume counter. She looked great. She has big bazooms."

Denny shot him a look of disgust. "You sure it was her?"

"What do you think, I'm stupid or something?" He turned away scornfully. Then shot Denny a glance over his shoulder. Smirking, he said: "Hey, Denny, if she's your sweetheart, how come you didn't know she was working at Kenton's?"

The bus appeared out of nowhere, belching and lurching like some kind of movie dinosaur, saving Denny the embarrassment of responding.

The moment she saw him, a big happy smile lit up her face and she beckoned him to the counter. He went straight to her and found himself immersed in a haze of smells, all kinds of perfume and cologne filling the air, making it seem as if she herself exuded the scents.

Her hair was pulled behind her head in a ponytail.

She was still beautiful, her smile radiant, just as he remembered.

"I'm so glad to see you," she said. "I was hoping someday I'd look up and there you'd be . . ."

"I've been trying to find you," he said. "I don't know your last name, only Dawn. I don't know where you live. So I couldn't call you. I hung around Barstow High one day after school trying to find you. I never did."

"I called you a few times," she said. "After school. But nobody answered. I even called from here once, on the pay phone in the mall. But the phone only rang and rang . . ."

All those calls he had not responded to in the afternoon, thinking it was that woman or the reporter and all the time—at least some of the time—it had been Dawn.

"I'm sorry," he said.

They stood looking at each other across the counter, the perfume surrounding them, too heavy and too cloying, but he didn't mind. A woman coughed, one of those attention-getting coughs, at the other end of the counter and Dawn made a small frown of apology at him and rushed off to serve her.

After a while, he grew uncomfortable standing at the counter—a perfume counter, of all places. Denny had a feeling customers passing through were eyeing him, either with suspicion or amusement. Suddenly conscious of his hands, he didn't know where to put them. He dared not look around to see who was looking at him. Without realizing it, he picked up one of the sample bottles of cologne and somehow pressed the little thingamajig, releasing a blast that smelled like lilac into his face, his eyes, blinding him momentarily and bathing his face. Blinking his eyes, he met Dawn's blue-gray eyes and they both laughed, even though he felt stupid.

Before a new customer could interrupt them, she told him her last name. Chelmsford. Scribbled her telephone number on a sales slip. "Call me," she said.

He left the store in a cloud of perfume, inhabited by scents he could not even identify, overpowering scents that made him slightly nauseated. Outside the store, he paused before crossing the street to the bus stop. Felt . . . what? He wasn't sure. He had her telephone number in his wallet. He could call her tonight.

He wasn't as happy as he had anticipated—he felt empty, in fact.

Glancing at his watch, he saw that it was almost three-thirty. Disappointment accompanied him as he waited for the bus that would bring him home too late for Lulu's phone call.

He didn't call Dawn Chelmsford that night.

Too much homework.

More than that: the telephone was next to the chair where his father watched television.

It wouldn't be possible to have a private conversation with Dawn Chelmsford within earshot of his father.

He'd wait to call her in the afternoon, when he got home from school and would be alone in the apartment.

But the next afternoon, he didn't call her, either.

*　　*　　*

"Would you like to know what I look like?" Lulu asked.

"Yes," he said, suddenly experiencing the usual leaping pulse and hammering heart.

"I'm taking a chance, you know," she said. Tentative now, almost teasing.

"What kind of chance?"

"Well, you might not like how I look. I might be tall and blond and you might not like tall and blond girls. Or I might be short and dark. And you might not like girls who are short and dark."

Taking a deep breath, he said: "I would like you, whether you were blond or dark . . ."

"Guess," she said. "Guess what you think I look like."

Another game, but a delicious one.

"Guess the color of my hair."

He thought of her smoky voice and said: "Black hair. Long black hair."

"Right," she said. "See? I think we were meant for each other, Denny. Now, what else? Do you think I'm tall or short? Or just about your height? When you dance with a girl and hold her in your arms, do you like her to be a bit shorter or as tall as you are?"

He'd only danced with a girl that one time, with Chloe at Bartlett. She was shorter than he was, fitted nicely into his arms. She was also the only girl he had ever held in his arms.

"A bit shorter than me," he said.

"Wonderful," she said. "That's me—just a bit shorter than you."

"Wait a minute," he said. "How do you know how tall

I am? Have you seen me?" A possibility he had not pondered in all his thoughts about her.

"Of course I've seen you. You may not like the way I look, but I love the way you look, Denny."

Thrilled again by her voice, her words, his body responded sweetly again. He was glad he was alone in the apartment, that she could not see him in all his confusion.

"Where? Where did you see me?"

"Someday I'll tell you that. But not now, Denny. Right now, we're finding out what I look like. For instance, am I pretty? Haven't you wondered about that?"

"It doesn't matter," he said. But it did, of course. He wanted her to be pretty—beautiful, in fact. As beautiful as her voice, as beautiful as the way she formed words with that voice.

"It matters, Denny. Because I want to be pretty for you. I want you to love my eyes, and my lips. I want you to love everything about me, Denny. I want you to love my body . . ."

That word conjured up wild thoughts and he was caught in a hurricane, gripping the phone fiercely, his palms wet.

"Want to know about my body?"

Unable to respond, he wondered whether she could hear his rapid breathing or his accelerating heartbeat.

"I have all the necessary parts. Some parts are better than others . . ."

"What parts?" he, astonished, heard himself asking.

"You'll find out," she said.

He wanted to ask more. But could not bring himself

to say the words, glad she could not see him at this moment, flustered and hot-cheeked.

"Next time I call, I'll have a surprise for you," she said.

He knew it was crazy, of course.

He was in love with a voice, with someone he had never seen, did not know at all, someone who might be a girl or a woman. Loved someone who was completely unknown to him, like someone in a dream.

Dawn Chelmsford was not a dream. She was real. She was beautiful. For a while, Dawn Chelmsford had been like a dream, out of reach, like all the other girls he had worshipped from afar—cheerleaders, girls in their bikinis on the beach or at a pool, lovely girls walking down the street who did not know he existed. Dawn had said, Call me. She'd said, I tried to call you. She'd said, I like the way you worry about the trees.

But Dawn Chelmsford was not the voice on the telephone. Dawn Chelmsford did not do things to his body and his mind the way Lulu did.

Am I some kind of crazy person? he wondered.

But all doubt was cast aside, postponed, as he lay curled up in bed, not wondering or worrying about middle-of-the-night phone calls now but holding himself, caressing himself, remembering her last words.

"Next time I call . . . I'll have a surprise for you . . ."

Later, in the far reaches of the night, the world hushed all around him, he could not sleep as those words echoed through his mind.

*   *   *

Hurrying into the driveway, running late, detained after classes for tutoring in math, Denny groaned audibly when he spotted the reporter from the *Wickburg Telegram* sitting on the steps of the porch, reading a newspaper.

A glance at his watch told him it was already after three-fifteen, that the telephone might be ringing at this moment.

The reporter glanced up and saw him.

Denny came forward, frowning, trapped.

"The story's all written," Les Albert announced, tucking the newspaper under his arm. "Except for the lead . . ."

Denny envisioned big black headlines, that old picture of his father on the front page. And everything that would follow.

"Know what a lead is, Dennis? Especially on a story like this? A lead determines the tone of the story, the mood, the theme. You don't have much choice with a straight news story. Like: twenty-two children dead. That's how a news story has to be written. But a feature story, now, that's entirely different. Know why?"

Denny did not answer, thinking: *twenty-two children dead.*

"Because, in a feature, you can control the story. Sure, you need the facts and the figures. I've done all that. It's all in the computer. When I have my lead, I can shift things around. Your father has got to be the lead, of course. Everybody else is gone. But how am I going to show your father? Still a suspicious figure after all these years? Still an unknown quantity? Or is he a good guy, after all? A family man, concerned for his wife and son? A martyr, sort of . . . It's up to you, kid."

"I've got to go in," Denny said. "I'm expecting an important call." Knew that sounded phony but couldn't help it. *Next time I call I'll have a surprise for you.*

"Tell you what, Dennis. I can give you, say, two more days. Then the story goes and I think all hell's going to break loose. Understand?" He reached into his pocket, brought out another card, a quarter Scotch-taped to it. "This is all you need. Today's Wednesday. Okay, Friday afternoon, call me collect at, say, three o'clock. We'll set up an interview. If I don't hear from you . . ." He sighed, tremulously. "I'm tired, kid. I work the night beat and I came all the way out here from Wickburg and my editor's on my ass." Denny was aware now of the gray face, the eyes bleary, probably with lack of sleep. "I'm not one of the bad guys, Dennis. I've got a wife and kids to feed. But I've also got a story to write."

The telephone was ringing as he opened the door to the apartment. He slammed it shut, racing for the phone, but the ringing stopped a moment before he reached it. He picked it up anyway and heard only the dial tone.

*H*er hand is on the telephone and I say, *Are you calling him again, Lulu?*

Why not, she answers. *It's all part of the plan, isn't it?*

It's more than just the plan, Lulu. It's what you're saying to him.

What am I saying to him, Baby? But she takes her hand away from the telephone, at least.

All those words. You're toying with him, Lulu, and he's just a boy. You're leading him on.

But I have to lead him on. To make him want to meet me, make him come to me.

Her hand is on the telephone again.

I think it's more than that, Lulu. I think you're having a good time. I think you're enjoying yourself saying all those things to him.

At first, anger flares in her eyes, then she slumps a bit and her face changes and it's long with sadness.

Is that a sin, Baby? To have a little fun, a bit of make-believe? Look at me. I've never had real love. Never had somebody hold me, caress me, feel my breasts. No one ever placed his tongue in my mouth. I've never lived, Baby. Never drove a car or held a job. Never took a taxi. Or went shopping for a spring outfit. Nobody ever winked at me across a room or asked me to dance.

Oh, Lulu, I say, my heart breaking into a thousand pieces. *I love you.*

But it's not the same, Baby. I love you, too. Aunt Mary loved us till the day she died but that's not the kind of love I mean.

I know, I say, thinking of our long bleak years together.

I am writing all this down now and Lulu is watching me. She finally comes to me, her shadow falling across the page, and she says, *Will you forgive me, Baby, for everything I've done and what I have to do?* and I tell her yes because she's my sister and we have been through so much together and I feel the old tenderness between us as she removes the roof that I hate, that makes my scalp burn like fire, and strokes my poor pathetic flesh while I keep on writing.

*T*he U.S. history class was boring, Mr. O'Keefe's voice droning on, tracing causes of the Spanish-American War which wasn't really a war. Windows open, slight breezes coming in, the smell of burning leaves from somewhere.

Denny's eyelids drooped. He stirred in his chair to keep awake. Looked up and around and straight into the eyes of Lawrence Hanson. Faint accusing eyes. Denny looked quickly away, disturbed, wondering why he was looking at him that way.

The bell brought the class instantly awake, as if a hypnotist had snapped his fingers. A rush for the doors as usual.

Slapping his books against his thigh, Denny came upon Hanson standing at the doorway.

"Have you got something to say to me, Colbert?" Hanson asked.

Denny shook his head. Guys squeezed by them in the usual mad rush to get from one class to another.

When the doorway was cleared, Hanson moved slightly, blocking Denny's way out of the classroom. "You look like you've got something on your mind," he said.

"You're imagining things," Denny said, feeling pinned down.

"I wish you'd tell me what's bugging you," Hanson said, as if he had all the time in the world, as if the bell for the next class would never ring.

Denny suddenly realized that something *was* bugging him about this guy. "Okay," he said. "That day under the bleachers—why didn't you fight back? You just stood there and let them push you around, let them hit you . . ."

"If I answer that, will you tell me why you ran away and didn't stop to help?"

Students now converged at the doorway, wanting to enter for the next class. One big guy, obviously a football player, shouldered his way between Denny and Hanson.

"Think about it," Hanson said, as the bell rang.

Denny did think about it. All during math, missing the homework assignment in social studies, sitting at the table in the cafeteria, isolated as usual from the other guys.

A few minutes later, he found himself wandering toward the athletic field, a place he'd avoided recently. He wasn't surprised to see Hanson sitting in the bleachers, all by himself in the vastness of the place. Somehow, he had known Hanson would be there, waiting for him.

Hanson didn't move as Denny approached. He didn't look up, either, although Denny knew that he was aware of his arrival. Denny sat down beside him. They both looked down at the field as if a football game was going on.

"I don't know what I'm doing here," Denny said. Which was the truth.

"Same with me," Hanson said. "But here we are."

"I know why I didn't stay around the other day," Denny confessed. "Do you know why you didn't put up a fight?"

"Sure," he said. "Those guys had been on my case since school started. I accidentally spilled a bowl of soup on one of them in the cafeteria. They started hassling me. They cornered me here that day. They wanted to fight. I didn't want to. What you didn't know about, Colbert, was this: I told them to take their best shots at me. I mean, they couldn't kill me, could they? So they pushed and shoved and knocked me down and got tired of it and walked away. Know what? I didn't figure I was the victim that day. They were. Those guys avoid me now, they look ashamed like they did something dirty. And you look at me almost the same way . . ."

Jesus, Denny thought, what's going on here? What kind of guy is this Lawrence Hanson, anyway?

"And I know why you didn't stick around, Colbert."

Denny didn't answer. He looked at the field, the grass scuffed from the practice sessions. He felt scuffed, too, as if someone had been practicing on him.

"You don't want to get involved with Normal, do you?" Hanson asked. "You don't look at anybody. You sit alone at lunch. You're worried about being exposed . . ."

Exposed caused Denny to look sharply at Hanson. A trigger word. Would a bullet follow?

"Your father, right? And that old disaster in Wickburg, at the theater there."

"How do you know about that?" Denny asked.

"It's no big deal. Normal's a small school. Word gets around. Everybody knows about what happened. So what?"

So what? He thought of Halloween next week and Les Albert's deadline tomorrow. "So everything," Denny said.

"Know what, Colbert?"

"What?"

"You've got a lot to learn."

That night, he couldn't sleep. Tossed and turned in bed, body weary but mind awake, filled with images. And voices. Mostly one voice: Lulu's. But the voice of Lawrence Hanson as well. *You've got a lot to learn.* Where do I begin? he wondered.

Finally, he got out of bed, put on his slippers and bathrobe, made his way through the shadows to the living room. Thought he'd have some orange juice, then decided against it. He sat down in his father's chair, near the telephone, letting his eyes adjust to the darkness. He stared at the phone, thought of all the calls his father had received in the middle of the night. Wondered what he would do if the telephone rang right now, this minute. Suddenly, he wanted it to ring, wanted to take one call for his father.

Looking toward the doorway, he saw his father standing there like a pale ghost in his bathrobe.

"What are you doing, Denny?" he whispered.

"I couldn't sleep. I've been sitting here like you for a thousand nights."

"Not a thousand, Denny." His father shuffled into the room, his slippers flapping on the floor. He sat on the ottoman, facing Denny. "What is worrying you, that you can't sleep?"

He thought of all the times he and his father had been together but had never really talked to each other. The other night, watching his father sitting up alone at the telephone, he had simply withdrawn and returned to his room. Although there was no connection, Lawrence Hanson's words came to him again: *You've got a lot to learn.*

"The guys at school, they know what happened at the Globe," he said. "That's what one of them told me today. And it's not a big thing with them. I thought . . ."

"What did you think, Denny?"

"I thought it would cause trouble. Like at Bartlett and the other places when I was a kid." His father looked frail, his face gaunt in the gloom of night. "Worse than that. I was worried about myself. Not you . . ."

"You should not worry about me, Denny."

But I do. Yet he'd never been able to tell his father that.

"You are sixteen, Denny. You should not have to worry about things like that. Your mother and I, we always tried to protect you from . . ." He sought the word, his hand trying to pluck it from the air. "From the world, I guess . . ."

"Sixteen, Dad. You were sixteen when it happened! You were my age." The knowledge overwhelmed him. He didn't know how he would have handled such a thing. All those children dead and all those accusations. But his father *had* handled it. Had endured, had survived. And all those years since then: *No comment.*

"Why don't you ever talk about it, Dad? Not only to me but to the newspapers, television. You answer the telephone and listen. You read the letters. You do nothing to protect yourself. Why?"

His father sighed, placed his hands on his knees as if about to get up. Denny was afraid he was going to avoid talking again, that he would tell him to go to bed, ending the conversation.

But his father leaned forward, his face close to Denny's.

"Maybe I was wrong, all these years, who knows? You do what you think is right, what you *feel* is right." Paused, sighed, shook his head. "Words, Denny, they never come easy to me. Contractions still a bother." Another pause. While Denny dared not move. "Those people, twenty-five years ago, the ones the children left behind. Fathers and mothers. The foster parents, sisters and brothers, what loss, what pain they felt. Time heals, like in the old saying. But for some, time does not heal. The pain stays, and it has to go someplace. It comes to me."

He closed his eyes. "So. Let them use the telephone, let them write me letters. Let them accuse me. Call me names. Worse—threaten. It makes them feel better. I offer myself up to them."

Eyes open again, looking into Denny's eyes. "Know what, Denny? Maybe I am guilty, after all. Maybe I should not have struck that match in the theater. More than that.

Maybe I should have investigated the balcony. But I hated to go up there. I was afraid of the place—the rats, the shadows. So, I confess my guilt, do my penance."

For the first time ever, Denny felt he had been admitted to his father's privacy, into a part of his life his father had finally trusted him to enter.

He wanted to fling himself into his father's arms, and knew that was impossible. But they had grown close in these few moments. It wasn't close enough maybe and there was a long way still to go, but it was a beginning.

"Go to bed now," his father said tenderly, not with his usual voice of dismissal. Concern, that the hour was late and another day waited tomorrow.

He stood at the public telephone in a cubicle outside the 24-Hour Store. The glass windows were smeared; the telephone book had been torn from its chain and taken away. He hated placing his lips close to the mouthpiece.

He inserted the quarter, pressed *O* for Operator. Told the impersonal voice that he wanted to make a collect call. Gave the number. The name: Les Albert. Listened to blurts of noise, and finally a woman's voice: *"Wickburg Telegram . . ."*

"May I speak to Les Albert?"

"Les is out right now. But he has a special answering machine. Want to leave a message—or shall I have him call you?"

He paused, frowning.

"He may be out most of the day on assignment," the woman said.

"I'll leave a message," he said. But *what* message?

The blurting sounds, followed by the voice of Les Albert, still tired-sounding. "Not available now, leave a message when you hear the beep . . ."

The blurt, the beep.

And Denny knew instantly what he was going to say, remembering his father, and joining him somehow.

"Mr. Albert. This is Dennis Colbert. Here's my answer: No comment."

Lulu did not call for three days. He dreaded the possibility that she might never call again. He paced the room, frustrated at his inability to call *her,* track her down the way he had searched the streets for Dawn Chelmsford.

Anger sometimes interrupted his disappointment. She was probably toying with him or teasing him. He recalled her voice, her words, words that set him on fire: *I want you to love everything about me.* The memory of those words always excited him. *I want you to love my body.*

If she did not call by four o'clock—and she had never called later than three-thirty—he'd leave the apartment and its loneliness, even though he was tired of killing time in the streets or at the library or the 24-Hour Store. Dave had been absent from the store during his recent visits.

"Is Dave okay?" he asked the clerk on duty. The clerk had gray hair and a high chirping birdlike voice.

"I think he has the flu," the clerk said, handing Denny his change, his hand birdlike, too, moving quickly in small jerking motions.

Denny slipped the Snickers into his pocket. Feeling

abandoned, lost. No Lulu on the telephone. No Dave in the store. The only people he could call friends.

And then, the next day: Lulu.

"Hello." Voice smoky as usual, thrilling.

"Are you waiting for my surprise?"

"Yes," he said. Something in her voice caught him, something he had never heard before.

"Are you sad?" Taking a risk.

Lulu did not answer immediately. He heard her soft breath, a sigh. "Everyone has sad days, Denny. You know that. Know what makes me not-so-sad?"

"What?" he asked.

"You. Seeing you. Would that be a nice surprise, Denny? You seeing me, me seeing you?"

Beyond his wildest dreams, something he had not thought possible, as if their relationship had no reality beyond these moments on the telephone.

"Yes, that would be nice, yes." Did he sound too eager, like a little kid?

"I can be with you Halloween night."

With you.

"How?" His mind racing. "Where?"

"Be at the corner of your street. Seven o'clock, trick-or-treat time." Pause, another sigh. "Wait for me, Denny. I'll be there . . ."

She hung up.

Leaving him in a state of utter bliss, except for the sadness in her voice, like the blemish on a perfect curve of cheek.

*　　*　　*

DEATHS OF 22 CHILDREN
HAUNT AFTER 25 YEARS;
BARSTOW MAN HARASSED

By Les Albert
Telegram Staff

On a quiet street in Barstow, Mass.—25 miles north of Wickburg—a man lives whose days and evenings are shadowed by a tragedy that occurred 25 years ago.

The man's name is John Paul Colbert.

The tragedy was the collapse of the balcony in the venerable Globe Theater in downtown Wickburg on Halloween afternoon, which took the lives of 22 children.

Cries of anguish still resound from that disaster, piercing the memory of countless people, including survivors and relatives of the victims.

Among those cries is a question that still echoes a generation later:

Does Colbert share the blame for that disaster?

Colbert, who was 16 years old and a part-time usher at the time, struck a match in the rubbish-strewn balcony, setting it afire moments before it crashed down as the innocent children below waited for a Halloween magic show to begin.

The official investigation cleared Colbert of any blame, citing the decaying condition of the balcony, which had been unused and neglected for many years.

Although he was never charged, accusations continue to plague Colbert's life. Through the years, he is reported to have received harassing telephone calls and hate mail, plus occasional death threats, including a bomb threat to his home.

Colbert has maintained a strict silence on the abuse. Whenever he is questioned, his exact words are: "No comment."

His son, Dennis, now 16, the age of his father at the time of the tragedy, continues in that tradition. "No comment," Dennis Colbert said this week when asked about his father's dilemma.

Meanwhile, friends and relatives of survivors still . . .

"Thank you, Denny," his father said, putting down the newspaper they had both been reading.

"For what?" Denny asked, his mind still dazzled by the parade of words on the printed page and his own name in black type.

"For 'No comment,' for respecting what I have been doing."

"I wanted to show my respect, Dad." *But I'm not you.* They looked at each other for a long moment. Then, Denny asked: "Will this story start everything all over again?"

His father shrugged. "Who knows?"

"The reporter didn't use our street address. Only Barstow. Barstow has a population of thirty thousand people. We had to do a paper on it at school."

"They have a way of tracking us down," his mother said. She had taken the *Telegram* from his father's hands and quickly scanned the story, after having refused to read it when the newspaper first arrived. "A sin," she had said, "bringing all this up again. Why can't they just write about the poor children, make it a tribute to them?" Then, looking at her husband: "Maybe we should go away this weekend . . ."

The telephone rang.

"We stay," he said.

Denny dared to do what he had never done before. He put his arm around his father's shoulder, and felt his father lean against him.

The telephone continued to ring.

Now, this moment: what he had been waiting for, standing on the corner, a shadow among other shadows, watching the parade of kids trooping by in the guise of ghosts and pirates and figures from the movies and television, Barney and Aladdin and one small girl in a bulging golden dress over her coat to protect her from the chill of the evening.

He spotted no one who resembled the monsters from the bus stop, simply because the children passed by in orderly fashion, no pushing or shoving, shepherded by someone older. Barstow was strict about Halloween trick-or-treating. One hour, between 6:00 and 7:00 P.M., and then home to empty all those paper bags of candy.

Denny glanced at his watch. Almost seven. Breathless, expectant, he checked out cars as they passed, his head swiveling like someone watching a tennis match. The neon lights of the 24-Hour Store down the street danced nervously in the air.

He had lied to his father about where he was going tonight. Told him that he wanted to take a bus to the library, where a Halloween program in the young adult room was being held. He saw his father wince, as always, at the mention of Halloween. Then, shrugging in resignation, he said: "Have a nice time." But typically, could not resist adding: "Be careful." Denny was both dismayed and elated to find out how easy it was to lie.

Without warning, from his blind side, a car pulled up, headlights sweeping the sidewalk, catching him in its glare. Blinking, he strained to see the driver, but saw only a dark shadow at the wheel. A dim hand beckoned, and he stepped toward the car, an old car, four doors, black, like a car in an old gangster movie. He pulled the door open.

The small bulb in the ceiling cast a feeble light as Denny slipped inside. Hand trembling with excitement—and nervousness—he closed the door, turned toward the driver and, astonished, saw Dave at the wheel. Without his roof, his skull inflamed, crazy tufts of hair sticking up all over, eyes deep with sadness, tight lips hiding the false teeth.

"I'm sorry," Dave said. "I didn't want this to happen. Lulu's my sister . . ." As if he had rehearsed saying these words.

A scent of perfume came from the backseat, as if someone had opened a fancy magazine. Hands slipped around his eyes, blinding him, soft flesh against his cheek, then that sultry telephone voice in his ear:

"Hello, Denny. I'm so glad we're finally getting together." Then, urgent and commanding: "Drive, Baby, drive."

The apartment they entered was cluttered, a confusion of cardboard boxes, clothing piled everywhere, bare walls pockmarked with ugly holes where pictures once hung. A transient look to the place, as if nobody had ever lived there or it was about to be abandoned.

Denny sensed that Lulu had not accompanied them into the house but he was reluctant to look behind him. She had remained in the backseat during the short drive to the apartment. Her hands had slipped from his eyes to the back of his neck then to his shoulders, touching him lightly.

Denny had managed to stay calm during the drive, simply because he trusted Dave. He was puzzled, yes, and nervous. Very nervous. His palms were moist, his thoughts in a whirl with a lot of questions—hell, a million questions—but he told himself to take it easy. Dave said nothing, concentrating on driving, his knuckles pale on the steering wheel. Lulu hummed a tune Denny did not recognize.

Dave now led him through a dark hallway to a closed door. Opening the door, he motioned Denny to step in, not looking at him, eyes downcast.

The first fingers of apprehension plucked at Denny. He had read somewhere that members of a jury never looked at a defendant when they were bringing in a guilty verdict, and Dave avoided Denny's eyes as he directed him to sit down in a straight-back kitchen chair. Except for two other identical chairs, the room was unfurnished, an unshaded bulb in the ceiling filling the place with naked light. Denny sat down tentatively on the edge of the seat, and turned, looking for Lulu, who was not to be seen. Finally turning to Dave, he was shocked. In the harsh, merciless light, Dave's face was red and splotchy, an ugly sore near his mouth, his eyes fevered and bloodshot.

"The Big One is back, Denny," he said. "Recess is over and the bell is ringing."

A clumping noise caused Denny to turn, and he saw a woman entering the room, leaning on an aluminum walker as she made her way painfully toward him, one deliberate step at a time.

"Hello again, Denny."

That voice. Lulu's voice. But this could not be Lulu, this woman with legs in steel braces, old, not old like a grandmother, but not young, skin tight on her cheeks, gaunt, disheveled black hair tumbling over her forehead in untidy bangs.

"Sorry to disappoint you, Denny," she said, the voice still husky but tinged with sarcasm now.

Denny's chest tightened; his throat constricted. He knew he had been fooling himself about Lulu, had known that she could not be the girl he had envisioned during those afternoon calls, but he did not expect someone like this—old and disabled, with bitterness pulling at the edges of her lips and a cold glitter in her eyes.

He looked toward Dave, not so much to see him but to take his eyes away from this woman who was Lulu.

"What's this all about?" he asked Dave. "Why am I here?"

But Dave didn't answer him, looked at Lulu instead.

"Let's not play any games, Lulu. If you have to go through with this, then do it right away."

Do what? Denny didn't really want to know the answer to that question. He just wanted to get out of there. He wasn't tied down, figured he could get up and leave at any moment. But some instinct told him it would not be as simple as that.

"Your father," Lulu said. *"That's* why you're here, Denny."

"What about my father?"

"Your father killed me. When that balcony crashed down. I died at the Globe Theater twenty-five years ago because of him." Did she say *died?* "He started that fire and the balcony fell and we died, me and all the others."

"My father wasn't guilty of anything," Denny said. "He was never arrested. There was no evidence against him."

"Cover-up," she said. "You weren't there. You didn't hear the screams. You didn't feel the pain. You didn't die the way I did."

A madwoman, Denny thought. *I'm getting out of this place.*

He made as if to rise from the chair but had no will to do it, his body not responding to his urgency.

A cold, crafty smile spread across Lulu's face. Harsh light glinted on the walker as she shuffled toward him.

"I don't think you noticed the tiny pinprick in the car, Denny. A small needle in your neck as we drove here.

170

Takes about twenty minutes to do its little job. I'm an expert with needles. You learn a lot spending time in hospitals, and I learned about needles. This was a special one. Keeps your mind alert but puts your body to sleep for a while."

She was right. He could not move. Or, rather, had no capacity to move. Wanted to, tried to lift his hands, tried to raise his body from the chair, but none of it suddenly seemed worth the effort.

"But no pain, Denny. I don't want you to feel pain. I want your father to feel the pain, the worst pain of all. The pain of losing his son and knowing he was to blame. That's the worst thing of all, Denny. Outliving your child . . ."

He felt doom descending upon him as the meaning of her words became clear. He knew now why he was brought here. For revenge—Lulu's revenge against his father. He looked at Dave, seeking help, but Dave's eyes were riveted on his sister, his body fragile, his hands clinging to his own chair, as if he'd fall if he had no support.

"What are you going to do?" Denny asked, trying to keep his voice normal, trying to hide the panic that streaked through his body, accelerating his heart.

"I'm going to be kind, Denny. I promised you no pain at all and I'll keep that promise. But I can't guarantee what happens after that. That's the sad part—what happens after you die . . ."

"What are you talking about?" Dave asked, speaking the exact words Denny wanted to utter.

"I'm talking about what you've always wanted to know, Baby," she said. "What happened when I died.

171

Now I'll tell you: My body was still as a stone. No heartbeat. No breath going in and out of my lungs. Dead! Want to hear the rest, Baby?"

"Yes," Dave said, rigid against the chair, eyes leaping with fever.

"Nothing," she said, voice flat. "Nothing, Baby. That's the horror of what happened to me. Worse than nothing! Becoming a blank! A terrifying blank! Unable to think and yet aware, knowing that I was a cipher and a zero. And, worst of all, my brain not working, only my awareness alive. That was the horror—knowing that I would be like this forever, for an eternity. No light at the end of the tunnel, Baby. No heaven and no hell. Or maybe *that* was hell, being a cipher in all that terrible blankness."

As she talked, her face became a blank, her eyes unfocused, as if she were not standing there in the room but had gone far away, someplace else. Then, back again: "Finally, it ended and I was trapped under the balcony. Alive again. Thinking. My bowels gave way and I lay there in my stench and my terror until they rescued me. But the terror was not from being trapped in the Globe but trapped in that eternity of nothing . . ."

Denny saw tears on Dave's cheeks, his face a mask of agony, mouth agape, his false teeth like small white bones jutting from his gums.

She did not acknowledge Dave's tears. Instead, she looked at Denny with those black eyes: "That's what your father did to me. To an eleven-year-old girl. Gave me a glimpse of horror, the worst horror of my life, worse even than these useless, helpless legs of mine."

A small twitching of his foot and a sudden tingling in his right hand gave Denny hope just when everything had seemed hopeless. His limbs were coming to life again. Maybe he had a chance of escaping this crazy woman, after all.

Dave reached out to embrace her, but Lulu shrank away from him.

"There's nothing out there, Baby. Now you know why I never wanted to tell you what happened. No matter what the priests or the ministers say, or those people talking about near-death experiences . . ."

"Maybe it was only a nightmare, Lulu," Dave said.

"Poor Baby, always trying to make things easy for me."

Denny could wiggle his toes. A cramp in the arch of his left foot was beautiful in its pain, signifying life and energy. His right arm felt as if insects were stinging it.

"If you want to make things easy for me, Baby, help me do what I have to do," Lulu was saying to Dave. Then, swiveling toward Denny once more: "Now it's your turn, Denny. To experience that terrible nothingness. Just a small pinprick and the beginning of sleep. Then nothing. Remember your father did this to you."

Denny didn't know where it came from, but a hypodermic needle suddenly appeared in Dave's hand. Lulu held out her hand but Dave withheld the needle. "It doesn't have to be this way, Lulu."

"There's no going back, Baby." Her hand still extended, palm up, waiting.

Denny poised himself to leap, placing his hands flat on

the chair on each side of his hips. Trying to get up from the chair, he found, to his horror, that he was unable to move his body, despite the surge of strength in his hands and legs. He was still trapped, his body caught in a strange inertia, refusing to obey the commands of his brain.

As he looked helplessly down at this body that was betraying him, panic in full sway now, he heard Lulu cry out: "What have you done, Baby?"

Glancing up, he saw Dave withdrawing the needle from Lulu's neck, saw a small worm of blood against her pale flesh, saw disbelief and horror distorting her face.

"I love you, Lulu," Dave said as she threw up her hands, losing her balance, then collapsing against the walker and stumbling over it, her hands grasping wildly for support and finding nothing to cling to. The floor trembled when her body struck it.

For one terrible moment, silence.

Still pinned in his chair, he watched as Dave knelt beside Lulu, cradling her in his arms. Bubbles of foam appeared on her lips; her body shook convulsively, then was still.

"I loved her," Dave said. "She suffered so much and didn't mean to be cruel."

"She wanted to kill me," Denny said, nodding at the hypodermic needle on the floor.

"My fault for letting it happen," Dave said. "I shouldn't have let it go as far as I did." He settled himself on the floor beside Lulu, holding her tenderly. "Get out of here, Denny. Please. Forget about us."

"I can't," Denny said. Meaning: he couldn't move and he couldn't forget.

"That drug must be wearing off by now. Stand up. Leave this place."

"What about you, Dave?"

Dave didn't answer, his hand stroking Lulu's face.

"What's going to happen to you?" Denny persisted.

Dave looked at him for a long, long moment, depths of sadness in his eyes.

And Denny knew what Dave was going to do.

"Please go, please leave us." Dave's voice now a whisper, weariness in every syllable.

Denny rose from the chair, robotlike. With movement came an urgency to leave this scene of sickness and death, get away from that demented woman dead on the floor and the ravaged man beside her.

He stumbled to the door on quivering legs. Bracing himself, he looked back, saw Dave's sad smile, those gleaming false teeth, saw him fumbling in his pocket.

"Good-bye, Dave," he said, closing the door gently behind him.

Outside, his body surging with strength in the brisk night air, he began to run, wildly and blindly, his heart keeping hectic pace, through the neighborhood streets.

Out of breath finally, pain clutching his groin, he paused at the telephone cubicle from which he had called Les Albert. After a while, he groped for a quarter in his pocket, placed it in the slot, heard the tumble of the coin in the mechanism, and prepared himself for what he had to say.

Later, he huddled in a doorway as an ambulance screamed past, a blur of white, followed by a police cruiser, blue lights twisting on its roof. He had not told the police dispatcher his name. Had told her what the police would find at the address he gave. He did not want Dave and Lulu lying abandoned and undiscovered in that apartment for hours or perhaps days.

He stood on the corner, looking at the neon sign of the 24-Hour Store down the street. The 4 was dark. Although cold, he stood there awhile.

He did not want to go home.

But there was no other place to go.

Maybe that's what home was supposed to be, he thought, turning into his driveway.

And you were lucky to have it.

*T*he monsters were acting up as usual at the bus stop, jostling and elbowing each other, calling out rude remarks to people passing by. A new monster had appeared, a kid no more than ten years old who stood apart from the rest, a sneer on his lips, along with a cigarette. He stood in a sort of half-crouch, revealing small sharp teeth when he inhaled. Denny searched his memory and labeled him Ygor II.

Looking up the street, he remembered the day—it seemed so long ago—that Dawn Chelmsford had arrived, and he wondered if she might show up again. He hadn't called her. He didn't know what he'd do if she appeared. She had become a pale presence in his life. But everything today was pale, like the early frost that had whitened windowpanes this morning.

Weariness tugged at his bones and muscles, and his eyes burned. He had not slept very much over the week-

end. The telephone had rung incessantly. Denny occasionally sat up with his father during the night hours, watching
as his father listened patiently, the phone pressed to his ear,
the lines in his face getting deeper as the night wore on. He
remembered his father's words, like a prayer: *I offer myself
up to them.*

Several times, he had wanted to snatch the telephone
from his father's hands and shout at whoever was at the
other end of the line, *Leave us alone . . . you must be some
kind of sicko . . . get a life.*

Some of the weekend calls had been from reporters, to
whom his father had repeated his familiar "No Comment."
Curious people walked by the house, craning their necks as
their eyes swept the building. Some took pictures. One
man wielded a cumbersome camcorder—maybe a TV
cameraman.

Denny had left the apartment twice during the
weekend. The first time was to walk by Dave and Lulu's
apartment. The house wore an air of vacancy, the
window shades pulled down, advertising circulars strewn
on the porch. The *Barstow Patriot* had carried a story
that day on the obituary page. The headline was stark
and blunt:

SUICIDE PACT
TAKES 2 LIVES

The story was matter-of-fact, not sensationalized like
in the supermarket tabloids. For the first time, he found
out Dave's family name—O'Hearn—astonished that he had
never bothered to ask what it was. He shook his head at
the sad, sad words: "There are no known survivors."

Denny knew it would be a long time before he would forget the events of that night. *Forget?* He would never forget. How close he had come to dying; the memory still caused his breath to catch. When he closed his eyes, the image of Lulu lying on the floor and Dave embracing her there came alive, like a movie in his mind. But real, not a movie at all.

Turning away from Dave's house, he wondered if he would ever tell his parents what happened. Maybe when the anniversary was over, the phone no longer ringing. Or maybe never. Maybe he'd forget it more easily if he never talked about it.

The second time he left the apartment was to accompany his mother to the early-morning six-thirty mass at St. Martin's. The church was almost empty. Kneeling in the fragrance of burning candles he thought about Lulu and the blankness. He wondered whether the blankness waited for everyone. He glanced at his mother, saw her praying devoutly, lips moving, eyes downcast. All the priests and nuns believed in heaven and hell and purgatory. Maybe the blankness *was* hell, as Lulu had suggested. He shuddered as a waft of cold stirred the air. He prayed the old prayers of his childhood—Our Father; Hail Mary, full of grace—the words automatic, but they filled his mind, took his thoughts away from Lulu and the blankness. Maybe the act of praying itself was the answer to the prayer. The thought caught him by surprise. It was something he would have to think about. Meanwhile, he kept on saying the prayers, over and over.

* * *

Now, as the bus heaved into view, Dawn arrived, in a rush, out of breath, swinging her bookbag.

She was still beautiful as she hurried aboard the bus, the monsters hooting and whistling but allowing her passage. Denny was the last to get on. He spotted her settling in a seat in the rear and made his way toward her, avoiding outstretched legs trying to trip him. Dismally, he saw that she had placed her bookbag on the seat beside her, the old signal that company was not wanted.

She was looking out the window as he passed by. He sat down two seats behind her. The bus lurched forward.

"Hey, Denny, your girl is back but I think she's mad at you." The voice of Dracula carried through the bus. Denny ignored him, as usual, concentrating on the advertising placards above the windows. "An Ideal Deal at Dealey's Auto Barn."

"Hey, Denny, how come you're such a loser?" That same Jimmy Cagney voice.

Right, Denny, how come you're such a loser?

He rose from his seat, was instantly thrown off-balance as the bus careened around a corner. He groped for support at Dawn's seat. She continued to stare out the window, but he saw color staining her cheeks.

"Watch out, Denny—she might take a whack at you." Dracula again.

"Would you?" Denny said.

She didn't look at him, but said: "Would I what?"

"Take a whack at me."

"I'm a nonviolent person," she said.

Finally, she did look up. "You didn't call," she said. Those blue-gray eyes were not angry but held a flash of—

what?—disappointment, maybe. Or hurt. He had never thought he was capable of hurting a girl that way.

"I read about your father in the newspaper," she said. "Is that why you didn't call? All that harassment stuff?"

A perfect cop-out: it would be so easy to lie to her. But he didn't want to lie. Not to her, of all people.

"No, something else. Something I can't talk about yet . . ."

She sighed, shook her head, muttered: "I must be crazy." Then pulled her bookbag off the seat and placed it on the floor.

He sat down beside her.

And found that he had nothing to say to her.

At Normal Prep, he stepped off the bus into a chilling wind that scattered leaves across the sidewalk. Guys streamed past him as he glanced dismally back at the bus, thinking of Dawn, thinking, *Damn it. Damn it! What's the matter with me?* She was beautiful and she'd made room for him on the bus—in her life—and he had sat there wordless, suddenly lonesome. For Lulu, of all people. For Lulu, who had tried to kill him, but lonesome for her anyway, for that voice on the telephone and the things that voice had said. *I think we were meant for each other, Denny.* How he'd loved that voice, loved even now the echo of it in his life. That meant he had loved nothing, loved nobody, because the Lulu who spoke those words to him had not been real, hadn't even been a ghost or a phantom, only a fantasy. *I want you to love everything about me, Denny.*

The first bell sounded. He trudged toward the gate,

books heavy in his arms. He spotted Lawrence Hanson hurrying along ahead of him. *You've got a lot to learn,* Lawrence had said. But how do you learn to say good-bye to someone who never existed?

The second bell rang. He walked slowly across the quad in November's cold wind, and went up the steps into the school.

Robert Cormier is a former journalist and the author of several brilliant and controversial novels for young adults. His books have been translated into many languages and have consistently appeared on the Best Books for Young Adults lists of the American Library Association, *The New York Times* and *School Library Journal*. He is the winner of the 1991 Margaret A. Edwards Award for *The Chocolate War, I Am the Cheese* and *After the First Death.* His most recent novel for Delacorte Press is *Tunes for Bears to Dance To.*